EMISSARY

- BOOK ONE OF THE EARTH EPSILON WARS -

TERRANCE MULLOY

Copyright © 2018 Terrance Mulloy
Tiny Empire Pty Ltd. All Rights Reserved.

This publication is a work of fiction. All characters, locations, and events are fictitious, and any resemblance to real persons, living or dead, is purely coincidental. No part of this publication can be reproduced or transmitted in any form or by any means, without written permission from the author.

For more information please visit:
TerranceMulloyAuthor.com

ALSO BY TERRANCE MULLOY

The Earth Epsilon Wars

Book 0: The Invasion

Book 1: The Emissary

Book 2: The Defector

Book 3: The Revered

Book 4: The Soldier (Coming Soon)

Audiobooks by Podium:

The Invasion

The Earth Epsilon Wars: Books 1-2

The Earth Epsilon Wars: Books 3-4 (Coming Soon)

Box Set by Aethon Books

The Earth Epsilon Wars: Books 1-4 (Coming Soon)

Stand-Alones/Short Stories

Rift

Alien Prison Ship

Enigma

TIMELINE

2048
The Wraith invade Earth.

2050
Mankind unites under the newly formed United Space Command (USC), and begins to fight back using captured Wraith technology.

2052
The Wraith suddenly abandon all battlefronts and retreat to their homeworld.

2054
The USC decides to pursue them, launching the biggest military counter-strike operation in the history of mankind.

2055
Utilizing the Wraith's zero-point-field technology, the first USC armada arrives at Epsilon 382-IV.

2065
With no victor in sight, the war still rages on...

CLASSIFIED | EYES ONLY
References: See Data Enclosure 1
USC Instruction (DoD/I) 5200.01

Excerpts from the personal journal of Dr. Michael T. Rossiter. Chief Virologist, USC Bio-Defense Counter-Measures Unit.

02. 18. 51:

"...It appears our invaders do share a lot of similarities to us. Aside from their humanoid appearance, their internal biology also seems similar. It's uncanny. And while I find *Homo Neoeuridius* abhorrent like most of us do, it's still fascinating to speculate about the origin of their species. The idea that two separate lifeforms could evolve on similar trajectories under vastly different environmental conditions is nothing short of astounding.

So, in conclusion, the average Neoeuridian (or *Wraith* as they are more commonly referred to) could almost pass as a human. However, I put a strong emphasis on the word *almost*. What ultimately gives them away is the hairless, pallid complexion, featureless grey eyes, and overall gaunt physical make up. This leads me to believe their species may, in fact, be dying somehow. Perhaps as a result of some environmental cataclysm, or possibly a genetic anomaly.

Over the past few weeks, I've also learned a great deal about how their inherent immune system works. Turns out there's a significant issue with the lymphatic system. Of the six deceased specimens I examined, each one also showed grave problems with bone mineral density - which reminded me of an extreme form of *osteogenesis imperfecta*. This could explain why their ground soldiers have those insidious-looking exo-suits fused to their limbs."

03. 25. 51:

"It seems each day we learn something new about these beings. Despite some of the biological similarities we may share as a species, what truly chills my blood is how their entire societal structure seems to center around a single Artificial Intelligence network. They allegedly call it, *the Combine*. Some in our intelligence community have speculated the Wraith view this AI like some omniscient deity, and that their society is enslaved by this technocracy. It's worth noting there's no actual proof of that yet. Truth is, as much as the USC loves to gloat about the reach of their covert operations and intelligence-gathering drones, we still hardly know anything about this Combine.

However, what is known, is that during battle it somehow autonomously controls each Wraith individually, either telepathically, or via some kind of embedded chip. This AI may also be organic in nature - meaning it could part of a much larger biomechatronic body. Of course, that theory too is speculation. But nevertheless, this is way more advanced than anything we have.

That worries me.

How do you outsmart something that is vastly more intelligent than you? I know this question keeps a lot of USC commanders awake at night."

04. 25. 51:

"It's very encouraging to know that something we suspected for months has now been confirmed.

While the Wraith may be ahead of us in molecular optics and communications, AI, stealth, and propulsion technology, it seems our pale blue dot has provided us with one major advantage over our invaders - a natural defense mechanism they did not account for:

Magnetoception.

The entire Wraith war machine relies solely on its AI to maintain communication and navigational networks, but for reasons we are still trying to understand, the Earth's natural magnetic field has begun causing absolute havoc for them.

Again, some of my colleagues have speculated that perhaps this has to do with the way the Combine utilizes sound to telepathically communicate. It is believed this AI can manipulate *phonons* - particle-like units of vibration that emerge from the complicated interactions of fluid molecules. These phonons also carry a slight negative mass, but the Earth's magnetic field cancels these encrypted sound waves as if it were a wi-fi signal being blocked.

In the last month alone, we've tracked entire fleets unable to coordinate their attacks and communicate with each other. Those not taken out by our own forces, hastily retreat to their primary staging base on the far side of the Moon. Even their orbital munition arrays now seem to be malfunctioning. It's a very strange phenomenon."

05. 02. 51:

"I realize the very act of me keeping this journal would be seen as insubordinate, perhaps even treasonous in the eyes of my superiors, but there are so many advancements happening, I feel it would be a crime not to chronicle this incredible moment in our history.

Today, I learned the various R&D units that were scrambling to understand the technology cache we captured from the enemy have made significant breakthroughs. The primary source of the Wraith's propulsion system is a zero-point-field reactor, which not only makes interstellar travel possible, but reliable and fast. And now, finally, USC engineers have been able to successfully implement these reactors into our own fleets. This has evened the playing field in ways we could never have imagined.

I'm also hearing about the huge ion particle, plasma, and electromagnetic scalar weapons being developed, capable of interfering with the anti-gravitational properties of their warships. This also plays into the persistent rumors that the USC is indeed preparing for something big. Possibly some form of a counter-strike.

This is all great news, and morale is high. But in any case, my little-known department continues to work hard to ensure humanity has at least one trump card left to play should the tide suddenly turn against us. My biggest fear is that the Wraith are waiting to reveal their *coup de grâce*, and in the meantime, want us to believe we are gaining ground.

But, I still carry hope.

Since I began my research here, I've discovered that despite their technological prowess, the Wraith harbor many biological vulnerabilities. They are highly susceptible to bacterial infections and disease - probably more so than we humans.

So, with a little luck, the USC won't even need these new super-weapons, as I am closer than ever to creating something far more lethal. Something that will eradicate the Wraith from existence..."

Final Entry/21.19/END_

ONE

April 02, 2065
Epsilon 382-IV. Camp Rhino
14 years after Dr. Rossiter's final entry…

IT WAS PRE-DAWN. Magic hour.

Epsilon's swollen Red Giant had only just begun to creep above the horizon when Sergeant First Class Matt Reeves entered the op tent. Even at this hour of the morning, the glare was close to unbearable for anyone not wearing their polarized sunglasses or faceplates.

Rhino's op tent was commonly referred to as *the Igloo*, due to the large filters that blasted cold air 24/7. It was a necessary and vital component for the troops stationed here. And while the tent was a welcome refuge from the murky humidity outside, it still offered very little relief overall as Epsilon's yearly climate was stagnant. There were no seasons, just perpetual swelter.

Matt had only walked a few yards from the main barracks and already he was drenched with sweat. He reached for his electrolyte flask and took a huge gulp as he stepped inside, nodding to a cluster of junior officers that were milling near the entrance. Matt noticed they each had *that* look in their eyes.

A look he knew all too well.

On average, it did not take long for Epsilon's thick, soupy air, endless coal-black landscape, and mustard-yellow skies to produce a negative physiological effect on any human unfortunate enough to be stuck out here on this hellish clump of rock. It was also no secret that some of the more high-ranking officers often referred to Epsilon as *the Bog*. It was an apt nickname.

Since arriving here, Matt often wondered if the great pioneers of space travel had gotten it completely wrong. Despite their bold and optimistic claims about how mankind was inevitably destined to reach the stars, now that mankind actually had, it was nothing short of a nightmare. A nightmare that many governments of Earth refused to acknowledge publicly. They also refused to acknowledge that the millions of troops and support personnel stationed here were struggling to keep this unprecedented war machine afloat.

Fun times.

As Matt surveyed the op tent, he figured this was going to be another overwatch briefing. For the past several months he'd been providing support to smaller ground-sweep units, but upon spotting several high-ranking officers from Darkhorse Battalion huddled in one corner, quietly talking amongst themselves, he knew something more elaborate was about to go down.

Hailing from Alpha Corps, Matt commanded a small off-shoot squad of Praetorians who called themselves, *Black Skulls*. Alpha Corps consisted of over fifty-thousand personnel from various elite military services around Earth, but none were more infamous than Praetorians. The U.S. regiment operated under an unorthodox chain of command that was largely made up of ex-Army Special Interstellar Forces and the Marine Space Corps. Praetorians dealt in covert rapid deployment. Their primary mission objective was to conduct full-spectrum recon and advanced combat operations on *dug in* enemy positions.

The United Space Command was a sprawling military bureaucracy, made up of over one hundred different countries. And while there was no shortage of elite fighters stationed on Epsilon and its four moons, what made Praetorians the envy of them all was the around the clock orbital munitions support. They could summon devastating ionized particle strikes from space at any time or hour, day or night, with a simple voice command. No other joint warfighting force had that capability. Praetorians were lauded as the deadliest and most effective regiment in the entire war effort. They were Gods of war.

At least they used to be. That was the good old days.

No regiment or squadron was afforded the luxury of orbital strikes anymore unless there was an extremely high-valued target or situation that warranted the expenditure. With USC resources under immense strain, drastic cuts were made with regards to mobility. Heavy space munitions across all fronts were reserved for special combat operations only. Anything not deemed a priority had to receive a green-light first. That meant smaller squadrons like Matt's now had to rely on other, less effective resources. Mostly AI piloted drones that had a habit of going AWOL in the field, and satellite imagery that was sometimes days old, at best.

Matt took a seat before the giant holoscreen that floated at the front of the tent, nestled between two members of his squad; Sergeant Alexa Hernandez, and Corporal James Kapernock.

The three other squad mates that sat behind them were Staff Sergeant Mike Pinehurst, Specialist Terry Strack, Sergeant John Gatehouse, and Specialist Lindsay Florez.

Initially, there were twenty-two hand-picked Praetorians assigned to Black Skulls. But in less than two months, fifteen had been declared KIA. Only seven remained.

This war was a motherfucker.

While they waited for the briefing to start, Matt looked around the room as more enlisted and commissioned officers from Darkhorse Battalion flooded into the tent.

It was nothing but polarized Oakley blades, bald scalps, and grizzled faces. Whether fresh meat or seasoned burnouts, every soldier looked haggard and battle-worn. Some of these guys were still wearing their combat armor having pulled back-to-back ops the night before, running on no sleep. The bald heads everyone sported was due to a bizarre form of head lice called *sesame seed*, which was prevalent on Epsilon. It was now standard practice for all ground troops and personnel to keep their heads shaved at all times.

"If we're going back out, maybe some of these greenies could pull security too," grunted Hernandez, as she ran her palm over her smooth, tattooed scalp. *Hell Hath No Fury* was scrawled large across the back of her cranium in ugly black ink.

"I'd say that's a given. Everyone in Darkhorse is turning up," Matt replied.

"Great. Another babysitting op," snorted Pinehurst.

"Nah, this is something else," said Matt, itching the stubble on his chin. "Something bigger."

Then, as if to punctuate Matt's comment, Lieutenant General Willard Hatchett entered the room.

Those sitting immediately stood. Those standing immediately snapped to attention.

Without even glancing at them, Hatchett motioned for the room to be at ease. "As you were."

Hatchett was a beast. A cob-nosed bulldozer of a man who was rarely seen around the base, yet his presence was felt everywhere. He was one of the most decorated officers here. He had also been given the seemingly impossible task of turning the tide of the war in this hemisphere back into the USC's favor. That meant he had no time for daily op briefings like this unless there was a damn good reason. The hushed murmurs that permeated throughout the tent added to everyone's bewilderment as to why this grizzled titan was here.

"That's Hatchett," Kapernock whispered as he took his seat again. "The hell's he doing here?"

"Seventy-seven Wraith kills," said Hernandez, her voice laced with awe. "All confirmed."

"It's actually ninety-seven," Matt replied. "He's even got the number tattooed on his forearm."

"I heard he was part of the first wave," Pinehurst said in a hushed voice. "Never left. Been in the Bog ever since."

Hernandez slowly shook her head, still in absolute awe. "Gotta respect that. Dude's a total meat eater."

The room dimmed for a split-second before the holoscreen lit up with an infra-red image of a Wraith operative crawling through a mottled swathe of black underbrush, its body clad in some type of camouflaged material. The ribbed, elongated muzzle of its rifle could also be seen, indicating this was most likely a sniper. The image was slightly pixelated, but it was unmistakably the enemy.

The Wraith had earned their foreboding nickname due to the advanced stealth technology they used, which allowed them to operate inside a light spectrum invisible to the human eye. Because humans can only see a small fraction of the entire electromagnetic spectrum, the USC had to quickly develop optical displays and scanning systems that could detect their thermal signatures.

Hatchett turned to face the room, his eyes betraying the hard glint of a man who had seen the worst of this war.

The room immediately fell silent.

Hatchett began. "Eight days ago, Kilo Company set out to establish a vital relay outpost in the Skrynn Valley. The company was a mix of combat engineers and technicians from three other battalions. They were tasked with constructing an echo-array network. As you know, these devices allow our orbiting fleets to communicate with ground forces and are also a crucial component in our enemy tracking apparatus. As you also know, installing them is highly dangerous - hence why they were accompanied by a small overwatch team of Praetorians. Our Destroyers softened up the area before they were deployed, but the moment they arrived, a Wraith sniper started picking them off. Last count, this sniper had taken out twelve of our guys."

Hatchett gave the room a moment to absorb the implications of that, then motioned to the image on the screen behind him. "We have reason to believe this sniper was somehow separated from its unit and was wedged into the area before we showed up. The Wraith won't conduct a rescue op until they're certain our orbital cannons are not positioned overhead, so they'll leave it to its own devices and hope for the best. Problem is, this one's a real snake. It's using some type of thermal blocking which is not standard issue. Every time we start tracking procedures, it disappears off our scopes. Every time it pops back up, it's in an entirely different location. Their Capitol is only several hundred clicks to the east, so we're not sure why this one continues to remain in the area. There's a chance it may be injured. There's also a chance it may be guarding something."

There was a pause from Hatchett as he clipped off the water flask from his belt and took a swig.

An officer from Darkhorse Battalion gingerly raised his hand.

"What is it, son?"

"Is it the Widowmaker, sir?"

Hatchett regarded the young officer with a measured stare before answering. "Maybe. Maybe not." A welter of soft murmurs broke out between the troops, so Hatchett pressed on before more hands could be raised. "At Delta Nova Time two days ago, Kilo Company went dark. All comms are down. Any attempt at hailing them is met with static. Now, I don't give a flying shit how good of a shot this sniper may be, I find it hard to believe it took out an entire company all by itself. Something else is going on out there. I want you to find out what it is."

Hatchett waved his hand and the image on screen flickered to an overhead image of the relay outpost location.

Apart from the construction equipment parked on the rim of a large hole, the entire area seemed eerily deserted. A volcanic wasteland of towering black mountains and razor-sharp cliffs. No visible vegetation. Waterless and windswept.

"As you can see, there are no visible bodies, which leads me to believe that a Wraith patrol swooped in, loaded them up, and hot-footed it out of the area before our surveillance drones showed up. We've had intel reports that suggest they are brazenly stealing our casualties right off the field - possibly an attempt to study our biological make-up. Could even be some type of long-term cloning program. Nevertheless, I want that entire region to serve as a tactical-assembly and staging area, so until that sniper is shut down, it continues to be a hazard to our day-to-day operations."

The screen then switched to a topographical map of the Skrynn Valley region. A series of animated waypoints were overlayed.

Hatchett continued. "Primary objective of today's mission will be to positively identify this sniper and engage it. Secondary objective will be to search for any members of Kilo Company and bring them home, dead or alive. Darkhorse Battalion will lead the charge with the assistance of Black Skulls. Your pilots are going to do two false inserts on the opposite side of the valley, and then you'll drop into the primary LZ to initiate sweeps of the area. Your bearing will be zero-three-seven, patrolling two kilometers to the designated layup point."

Hatchett pinched the air and the screen zoomed into a cliff face near the landing zone. "You will advance up the side of this cliff face, which will offer good concealment. The terrain is going to be extremely rocky, so be sure to lace up and watch your footing. You fall into a Hellsting nest, no one's gonna come for you. Once the area is secured, you will hold the perimeter and set up a temporary base until a construction echelon can join you. I'll do my best to wrangle up some Destroyer support if needed, but with over three-hundred active fronts being fought across this system, I don't need to remind any of you how thinly stretched our elements are right now. That's including our QRF units."

Thick silence blanketed the room as looks were traded among troops. *This was going to suck.*

Hatchett clicked his fingers and the holoscreen vanished. "All comms will be relayed through Archangel; call sign is Warhammer. Crypto will be wideband, segment X-twenty-two. Entire region is steep with highly magnetized minerals, so expect typical interference problems. Regardless, we'll be on a one-hour comms window."

Another officer from Darkhorse Battalion raised her hand. "Can we expect more than one unfriendly to show up?"

"I would," Hatchett said, his voice devoid of any emotion.

"Rules of engagement?" she replied.

Hatchett almost smiled at that. There was only one rule of engagement in this war: *kill anything that wasn't human*. "Should any additional Wraith units turn up, you have my permission to get bloody." His gaze shifted, surveying the room with the steely confidence of a man who has commanded millions of men and women into battle. "Remember, set your faceplates to full tint, and drink lots of electrolytes out there. Any more questions?"

There were none.

"You roll at 0500. Good luck."

And with that, everyone began filing out of the tent.

Hernandez turned to Matt and Kapernock with a shit-eating smirk. "Ducks in a barrel. Let's kill some Wraith."

Matt leaned over and bumped fists with her.

TWO

THE BLACK SKULLS trailed closely behind Darkhorse Battalion, both dropships streaking over the treacherous expanse of gnarled rock. They were two hundred clicks from Camp Rhino, heading straight towards the Skrynn Valley - the heart of Epsilon's badlands. Out here, the sulfur pits were known to glow orange like lava.

Matt sat in the rear open cabin, elbow-to-elbow with what remained of his team, thinking about how much he was going to miss them.

He had recently turned forty-two and was nearing the end of his tour. Six years in total. One year in cryostasis, hurling across the gulf of interstellar space, and four-years of active duty in the field, fighting the bloodiest war in the history of humanity. And then, assuming he somehow survived all of that, another year traveling home, hoping he wouldn't drown or freeze to death in his sleep.

A small-town cop in his previous life, Matt joined the USC after surviving the invasion, or *World War Wraith* as it was most commonly known. This was an unfinished fight he could not back away from, especially after losing his wife, Karen. But now, being light-years away from Ally, his ten-year-old daughter, it was all starting to grind on him, both physically and emotionally. Matt was done with this war.

He turned to the soldier nearest to him, Strack, who was struggling to keep his breakfast down. "You puke in your helmet, you're in for a helluva day," he yelled over the high-pitched drone of engines.

Strack nodded in agreement, breathing in the heavy side-wind that buffeted their cabin. "Forgot to take my goddamn motion sickness pills this morning."

"That's the third time this week, bro," said Kapernock with a wry smile. "A tell-tale symptom of early dementia."

Strack looked at him inquisitively before sucking down another deep breath. "If it's dementia, does that mean I'll soon forget what your ugly face looks like?"

Hernandez looked up at them and scoffed. "You really think you're gonna forget Kapernock's ugly face? That shit is unforgettable."

Kapernock blew her a kiss.

Hernandez just shook her head and looked away.

Florez killed the heavy metal music that was pounding through her helmet and looked up at Strack while adjusting her armored wrist plate. "Just so you know, Commander Spot, you spit up anywhere near me, I'm gonna toss your ass outta this dropship myself."

The other soldiers chuckled.

Matt also couldn't help but grin. Strack was a dorky mid-western kid whose acne-pocked complexion found little relief from Epsilon's humid atmosphere. While Matt never addressed him by Commander Spot, he liked the idea that Strack considered it a term of endearment more than an insult. Plus, the multitude of skincare products and lotions he kept back at base also supplied the squad with enough joke material to last a lifetime.

Matt heard a low-rumbled splutter from Darkhorse's dropship in front of them. He turned his head and kept his eyes trained on it.

The older TJ-1822 models were clumsy-looking slabs of reinforced metal that rumbled through the air, spewing electrified discharge from their grimy underbellies. From this position, which was slightly above Darkhorse, Matt could see all the troops in the rear cabin, jammed together like canned sardines.

"Hey, Gatehouse, you really think it's the Widowmaker out here?" yelled Hernandez.

"Like Hatchett said, who cares?" Gatehouse replied, his dark features bathed in an electronic glow underneath his faceplate. "As long as we take that sniper out, it's all good, baby."

"Yeah, well, I would still love to get me a shot lined up. They say he's killed more of our troops than any other Wraith in the field."

Gatehouse grinned at Hernandez. "What makes you think it's a *he?*"

Hernandez shrugged. "Just a hunch. No female, Wraith or human, would be stupid enough to stay alone out here for days. If a Hellsting doesn't find you, a bad case of sesame seed would."

Gatehouse chuckled while checking the adjustable grip attachments on his long-range sniper rifle. "Whoever that sniper is, if there's a clear shot, it'll be me who takes it."

"Not if you end up dead before me."

Gatehouse shot her a stink-eyed look.

Hernandez grinned and raised her middle finger.

Gatehouse roared laughing.

"Gatehouse, no offense, but how the hell can you still see anything?" said Pinehurst. "You're old enough to fart dust."

Gatehouse turned to Pinehurst with a shit-eating smirk. "Got the magic eye, I guess."

"You mean a *fake* magic eye," sneered Hernandez. "How much did those aug-enhancements cost?"

Gatehouse shrugged. "No idea, the USC paid for them."

Hernandez and Pinehurst both shared a look and snickered.

Gatehouse caught them and smiled. "Guys, come on. Be honest, what's cooler than a USC scout sniper with augs?"

"Blowing shit up," replied Hernandez. "Blowing shit up is way cooler."

"But you're not an EOD tech."

"My older brother was. Earned his crab-badge the first month he arrived here. His ordinance unit was assisting a French battalion when they got cut off by a Stalker. Crazy bastard managed to Frankenstein a directional charge together out of a can of chickpeas and several cobalt ammo cartridges. Almost blew the damn thing back to Earth."

"Are you shitting me?"

Hernandez looked at Gatehouse, serious as cancer. "I shit you not, soldier."

Gatehouse groaned. "Hernandez, how many times do I have to tell you, I'm not a soldier. I'm a Marine... or at least I was until I got assigned to you lot."

Hernandez laughed. "What you are or were doesn't mean shit on this rock, Gatehouse. You're just cannon fodder like the rest of us."

"Go fuck yourself, Sergeant."

"Gladly. But not before I take out the Widowmaker."

Gatehouse and Hernandez met eyes again.

She winked at him.

He grinned. This type of sparring match was a regular occurrence between them.

"You guys are assuming someone else hasn't taken out the Widowmaker already," said Strack, as he slid up his faceplate to shove a stick of raspberry gum into his mouth. "If he's still alive, there's probably a huge price on his head by now... or hers."

"The hell you on about?" grumbled Florez.

"You didn't hear?"

"Hear what?"

"Apparently, the USC allowed a whole bunch of private contractors to hitch a ride from Earth on that last rotation. So don't be surprised if we come across some other thumpers roaming around out here aside from ourselves."

Florez curled her lip. "Man, that is some bullshit right there."

"You can say that again," said Gatehouse, nodding in agreement. "What, USC suits worried we can't do our job anymore?"

"Hey, it's what I heard, is all I'm saying. No one is confirming it's true." Strack contunued chewing ferociously as he shoved another stick of gum into his mouth. "But considering how fucked up things are here right now—"

"Get that faceplate shut, Strack," ordered Matt. "We fly through a grit flare, you'll lose both your eyes."

"Copy that," he replied, HUD readouts flickering to life as he lowered his faceplate.

The pilot's voice suddenly boomed into their audio feeds. *"Approaching LZ. Sixty-seconds."*

"Map up!" barked Matt, tapping the side of his helmet.

The others followed suit. Streams of new data lit up across their faceplates as the surrounding terrain began to be mapped in three-dimensional real-time.

Then, an alarm started bleating throughout the cabin indicating the dropship was descending to land.

"Safety latches off," yelled Matt. "Prepare to discharge—"

Thwack-Thwack-Thwack-KA-BOOM!

The shockwave from the explosion rippled over Matt and his team with a deafening crack. The violent jolt caused everyone to snap their attention to Darkhorse's dropship.

To their horror, it was careening recklessly down to the surface, white-hot flame belching from every vent and crevice. Wraith artillery strafed the air as burning soldiers leaped out of the rear cabin to meet their deaths below. Some were violently tossed out, others clung to the hull for dear life, their bloodcurdling screams drowned out by the dropship's failing engines as it spun out of control.

Strapped inside a windowless, sub-nosed cockpit, using a virtual display attached to an augmented headset, the pilot began firing the gimbaled pulse cannons that were fixed to Black Skulls' dropship. Exactly what he was firing at was unknown, as there were no visible targets to acquire, despite the optimal situational-awareness the real-time overlays and drone feeds provided him. The pilot was firing out of sheer panic. *"Black Skulls, you need to hit your silk!"* he screamed over comms.

Matt punched a large red button on the side of his seat.

There was a hydraulic whine as the cabin floor dropped away. Their legs were dangling over a five-thousand-foot drop, the terrain below, rushing past at seven-hundred miles an hour.

Matt wheeled to his team. "Deploy chutes! Detach now!"

But none of them managed to hit their harness releases.

Their dropship was struck by two searing-hot lances of charged ion particles.

The first artillery strike severed the primary engine and the cockpit shell, rendering any aerodynamic properties the vehicle had as utterly useless. The second strike smashed into the rear hull, peppering Gatehouse and Florez with shrapnel. Insane G-forces kicked in as the dropship started tumbling to the surface at terminal velocity. The cabin floor sealed shut again, a warning beacon droning as automatic safety protocols kicked in. But it was to no avail. They were going down faster than the ship's navigational systems could compute.

Screams and fire everywhere, Matt's faceplate flashed neon-red, indicating they were about to hit something any second. Fighting the sickening G-forces, he managed to turn his head to see the rocky terrain rushing up to meet him.

It was at that moment he blacked out.

THREE

MATT WAS AWAKENED by Pinehurst gently nudging his shoulder. "Matt, you in one piece? Matt!"

Matt's heart hammered against his aching ribs, and his head throbbed like a jackhammer. "Goddamn that sucked," he muttered, his nose packed with dirt, his mouth filled with the coppery tang of blood.

He slowly opened his eyes to see Pinehurst hovering over him with concern. But something else was wrong. Pinehurst was weirdly flickering and shifting into multi-colored fractals. It was then Matt realized his faceplate was cracked, and the HUD was malfunctioning.

He peeled his helmet off and tossed it aside, his eyes squinting from the harsh glare of the sun. "I— I need a sitrep," he croaked. Everything felt lopsided as he involuntarily gulped in a lungful of smoky air that made him cough. The hot air stunk of burnt metal and smoke.

"We came down hard, but we stayed intact," replied Pinehurst. "Would've been a lot worse if we didn't clip that bluff on the way down. Broke our descent. We skidded the rest of the way. Fire's mostly out, but... we've got casualties."

Matt painfully unclipped himself from his buckled seat, taking in the wreckage. His upper lip was bleeding. He probed it with the tip of his dry tongue and winced. The cut was deep. "Pilot?" he asked.

"Killed on impact."

Matt breathed a defeated sigh. Then, he spotted Gatehouse.

He was still strapped into his seat, head slumped, minus his helmet. His right cheek had been blown away - the wound deep enough that the white of his jaw and cheekbone was visible. The opposite side of his scalp was a lacerated mess, and there was a thick clump of blood that had pooled in his lap.

Next to him was Florez. Or at least what was left of her. Her torso had been severed in two - her exposed stomach entrails glistening in the sun, dangling across segments of her shattered body armor like ropes of sausage.

Kapernock and Strack were busy attending to Hernandez. Her left thigh had been impaled by an overhead girder, pinning her to the troop seat. Matt noticed the color had drained from her cheeks as she sat there, writhing in pain. The whites of her eyes were also stained red where the capillaries had ruptured.

Kapernock carefully clipped off her shin-armor. Her entire leg was wet with dark blood. Not a good sign. Strack quickly prepared a hefty dose of morphine from his own field-kit.

"I don't wanna feel a damn thing," she said, grimacing through the agonizing pain.

Strack plunged the small field-needle into her upper leg. "You won't."

Hernandez gave a weak moan and her head lolled forward.

As Matt watched them work on Hernandez, a wave of grim certainty settled over him, robbing him of any movement. *Aside from himself, only four of his squad remained. He had lost nearly all of them, and yet somehow, he was still alive.*

Pinehurst turned to Matt and saw the vacant look in his eyes. "Matt, you checked to see if anything's broken?"

Matt blinked out of his train of thought and began to check himself over, his armor bashed and cracked, his eyes struggling to remain open from the sun's merciless glare. He wiggled his fingers underneath his breastplate, igniting a constellation of pain. But still, nothing felt broken, just deeply bruised - possibly sprained. "I don't think so... nothing feels broken," he mumbled vacantly. "My ribs and chest are pretty sore, but... only a busted lip."

Kapernock moved to Florez and gently took the helmet off her slumped head, handing it to Matt. "Here. You'll need this."

Matt gave him a taut nod and slipped it over his head, tapping a small side-panel to reset the HUD. It flickered to life as it cycled through its default start-up code, highlighting nearby friendlies. Then the faceplate darkened, shielding his eyes from the sun's glare. "We can't be out here. Hernandez needs immediate evac. Strack, call in a QRF unit."

"Already have."

"What'd they say?"

"Have a nice wait. We're looking at least a five-hour ETA before anyone can reach us."

Matt could feel the pit of his stomach tightening. He figured they needed to round up as much ammo as they could, and dig in for the wait. Five hours in USC time often meant six or seven. Sometimes longer. There was even a chance they could be out here all night. With a little luck, the Wraith wouldn't show up until they had already evacuated. Matt knew that was unlikely. Even though the artillery strike probably came from many miles away, perhaps as far as the opposite side of the planet, a clean-up crew would almost certainly be inbound to investigate both wreckages and eliminate any survivors.

Matt allowed his eyes to drift over the twisted clumps of metal and debris that surrounded him.

Despite the impact damage, the dropship's rear cabin was mostly intact, offering substantial cover. But until support arrived, they were nothing but sitting ducks out here.

Wherever *out here* was.

FOUR

MATT CRAWLED over to the lip of the cabin and pulled himself up to view the barren terrain.

They were at the bottom of a narrow valley, both sides framed by towering cliffs of sharp rock. While they were in the designated region, according to Matt's HUD, the insertion point was about three miles to the west.

In the distance, Matt could see what remained of Darkhorse's dropship through the rippling heatwaves, smoke drifting in dead gales over the wreckage. And soon the *Scavs* would come - vulture-like predators that had no shortage of dead flesh to feast upon since the war began here.

This is a bad spot, he thought. But regardless, he needed to reach that wreckage and search for any survivors. "Pinehurst."

"Yeah."

"Think you could hold the fort for a few hours?"

Pinehurst looked out at the thin column of smoke in the distance and shook his head grimly. "Matt, they've all gotta be KIA. There's no way any of them could have survived that fall. You saw that ship, it was a fucking meteor before it even hit the ground."

Matt kept his eyes on the desolate valley before him. "I still need to check it out. Besides, we could use the extra ammo and supplies."

Thwunk!

Suddenly, an ionized round punched into the hull, inches from Matt's head. He ducked and spun to the others. "Sniper! Get down!"

Pinehurst, Kapernock, and Strack dropped to the floor of the cabin, snatching their assault rifles.

The thick air began to sing as a flurry of plasma rounds rippled across the gap between the valley and the dropship wreckage, cracking into the cabin.

Thwunk!

Thwunk!

Thwunk!

Thwunk!

Then, the cascade of bullets halted as suddenly as it started.

Matt kept his back planted firmly against the cabin wall, straining to listen over the blood throbbing in his ears. "I think it came from in front of us," he hissed, clawing for his own rifle.

"That's gotta be the Widowmaker!" said Strack.

Matt was thinking through their next move when he caught sight of the blood still dripping from Hernandez' leg. She needed to get properly stabilized, ASAP. "You three stay on Hernandez, I'll deal with this," he said.

Hernandez was unable to move. Now in an opiate-fueled haze, she chuckled as another salvo of rounds punched the cabin. "That better not be the Widowmaker," she sneered, sluggishly reaching for her rifle, but unable to grasp it. "Don't even think about taking him out. He's mine. Especially you, Kapernock. Remember, bitches get stitches."

"Hernandez, please do me a favor and shut the fuck up! And stop trying to move!" Kapernock snapped.

Hernandez responded with a care-free snort, her glassy eyes struggling to stay open.

Strack examined the girder protruding from her thigh. Despite the makeshift tourniquet they had applied to her leg, the bleeding had not slowed by much. "How're we gonna get her leg free?" he said, yanking on the girder.

That caused Hernandez to groan. "The hell, Strack?"

"You felt that? You've had enough morphine to knock out an elephant."

"Doesn't mean I want *you* messing with my leg," she slurred back to him.

"I wouldn't pull on it," suggested Pinehurst. "She could still bleed out."

"Dude, she *is* bleeding out." Strack motioned to her blood-drenched leg. "Tourniquet didn't do shit."

Matt looked up, suddenly remembering a paragraph he had once read in an operations manual. USC protocol stated that at least one fully stocked medical-kit was to always be kept in a storage cache at the front of every dropship cabin. These kits were also built to withstand intense damage, such as enemy fire and crash landings.

Matt wheeled to the front of the cabin where a ribbed-container could just be seen among the debris, about the same size as a cooler. It was battered and charred, covered by a tangle of shredded steel, but still intact. Matt clicked his fingers, eagerly pointing at it. "Kapernock open that storage cache. Strack, Pinehurst, give him a hand. If there's a blow-out kit in there, we should be able to cut her free and shrink-seal the wound."

"Roger that," said Strack, following Pinehurst as they belly-crawled over to help Kapernock. There was plenty of debris that was covering the container, and it would take the three of them to clear it.

Pinehurst was crab-walking on his elbows when another enemy round hit the cabin, just several inches above him. "Shit!" he yelped. "This guy must have a lock on us somehow."

"If he did, you'd already be dead," said Kapernock. "The whole ship is coated in that thermal-blocking stuff, so he can't see our heat-sigs. He's just taking random pot-shots."

Matt had to find a way to take this sniper out. To do that, he needed to locate its position. He leaned over and began searching through Gatehouse's blood-soaked Velcro pouches, pulling out a retractable target-spotting device. It had a small mirror attached to the tip of it. It was no longer standard issue to have a manual device like this, but despite Gatehouse's augmented eyes, he was old school. Whatever the tool, if it worked, he'd use it. And sometimes, all he needed was a small shaving mirror to get an angled view of a distant enemy target or position.

Matt extended the device's pole and slowly raised it over the lip of the cabin, tilting the mirror slightly downward to get a look at the distant cliff faces.

Twhap-crackkkk!

The device was violently flung out of Matt's grip when a round shattered the mirror to dust. Matt recoiled with a sharp breath, yanking his hand away as if he'd just been stung by a wasp. "Oh, you cheeky mother—!" Without the ballistic nano-padding inside his armored glove, he would have lost all five fingers from the ricochet of that shot alone, possibly his entire hand. He breathed a sigh of relief, but still wiggled his fingers to check none were missing.

He huddled there for another moment, thinking through his options. There was only one, and it wasn't good. He had to draw fire again so he could get a lock on the sniper's position. "Popping smoke!" he yelled, clipping off a smoke grenade from his belt.

"Copy that," said Strack, holding the badly dented storage cache with Pinehurst while Kapernock cracked it open to retrieve the med-kit inside.

Matt rolled the grenade along the floor in front of him. Smoke began to spew from it, clouding the cabin. Then, he reached for Gatehouse's sniper rifle, waiting until the haze was thick enough. He'd be exposed, but hopefully only for a few seconds. He popped up, his right eye glued to the large scope as he scanned the valley in front of them.

Thwunk!

Another round clipped a support girder next to his head,

knocking Matt backward as if he'd been kicked by a horse. With the smoke still thick, he scurried to his feet and popped up again.

Matt figured this sniper had to be at least a mile out. Maybe further. It was not only firing blindly but also impatiently. That implied it was most likely suffering from fatigue. Matt also suspected this was not the famed Widowmaker. Whoever this sniper was, it seemed sloppy - almost like it was goading them.

Matt continued to scan the valley. He couldn't see anything from all the smoke, but he didn't need to. All he needed was a few more seconds for his rifle scope to complete its area scan and get a hit on the source.

"You're pushing it, Matt," warned Pinehurst. "This guy's eventually gonna luck-out and spot your big ugly head."

Pinehurst and the others had broken open the supply cache and found the med-kit inside. There was a vast array of medical gear and field devices; everything from gauze, sutures, surgical instruments, antibiotics, syringes, even a small laser cutter. They got started on freeing Hernandez.

Kapernock scoffed to himself, shaking his head while he readied the laser cutting device. The thin blue flame ignited, causing the translucency on everyone's faceplates to automatically thicken. "I tell you, if the Wraith didn't decimate our military AI all those years ago, we wouldn't even be out here dealing with this shit. The USC would've just sent a bunch of drones and unmanned exo-rigs to fight on our behalf. Meanwhile, I'd be kickin' back at Wrigley with a chili dog and a Coors Lite."

"You mean, you'd be kickin' back at what's left of Wrigley," said Strack.

Kapernock looked at him as if he'd just blasphemed. "Wrigley Field's still standing, bro. Even these assholes couldn't knock her down entirely."

"But you're not even from Chicago. You told me you grew up hating the Cubs."

"So?" Kapernock shrugged before he began cutting through the girder. "I'd still love to be there right now. Better than this fucking place."

Matt's HUD suddenly pinged with a signal. The rifle scope had located the target and its distance from them. It relayed the calculations to the internal tracking system in Matt's helmet. "I got something..." He ducked down again, a stream of fresh data flooding across his faceplate. "OK... target is north-east... seven-hundred and forty-two yards out."

"That's over four miles," snorted Kapernock. "Not even Gatehouse could've made that shot."

Matt looked down at the oversized scope attached to Gatehouse's rifle. Kapernock was right. Even with zero wind, it would be an impossible shot. There was only one way he could get to that sniper and shut it down. He would have to head out on foot and find a way to flank its position without being spotted.

Pinehurst watched as Matt began surveying his ammo and gathering extra supplies from his deceased squad mates. "Matt, Hatchett said that sniper was using some type of special cammo. That lock you just got could be a false target. A decoy."

"Only one way to find out." Matt gave the supply pouches that were strapped to his armored suit a quick check over. "I want you to hold the perimeter until I get back."

Pinehurst glared at him incredulously. "Maybe you should stay here until our QRF arrives."

"I need to check that Darkhorse wreckage for any survivors. Then I'm going to take out that sniper. Unfortunately, to do that, I'm gonna need to get closer to him. A lot closer."

"And you think going out there alone is a good idea?"

"No. But unless you have any other ideas..." Matt took a deep breath, shoving three ammo cartridges into a side pouch. "Figured if I haul ass I could reach it in just under an hour." Matt tapped a small console on his forearm and flicked a small ball of light over to Pinehurst.

The HUD on Pinehurst's faceplate started blinking, alerting him of the new data Matt had just transferred across to him.

"I know it's wishful thinking, but use those coordinates and call up a strike. The Widowmaker is a high-priority target. Maybe we'll get lucky and command will reroute a Destroyer to this grid."

"Right, and if you head out there, you'll be directly within its strike zone."

Matt gave Pinehurst an exhausted look. "Hopefully I'll be on my way back by the time that happens. That's assuming it even does happen."

Pinehurst swallowed his dry throat. He didn't like this plan. "Maybe I should go with you."

"Nope. I said I want you here," Matt replied in a sharper tone.

Pinehurst watched as Matt rummaged through Hernandez' supply sack, pulling out a small shape-charge and bagging it. "What if a Wraith patrol turns up?"

Matt turned and met Pinehurst's glare. He could see he was both fearful and irritated. "You do what you can to hold this perimeter."

Kapernock paused from the girder he was cutting and looked up at Matt. "And how are we supposed to do that with just three of us?"

"Set your fire to three-round bursts. Don't waste your shots."

"Gee, thanks. That's comforting to know," Kapernock mumbled under his breath as he went back to cutting the girder.

Matt held out his fist for Pinehurst to pound. "Just make sure you get Hernandez stable before she wakes up."

Pinehurst nodded and pounded Matt's fist. "And you just make sure you get your scrawny ass back here alive… sir."

Matt couldn't help but flash a grin. Out of all his squad mates, Pinehurst and he were the closest. Matt first met him in a chow hall when they were prepping for interstellar deployment on the USC Lexington. *"Dude, we'll probably die in stasis before we even reach Epsilon,"* he said to Matt with a shit-eating smirk as they were both climbing into their cryo-pods. *"You know these cheap-ass pods are all made in China, right?*

Apparently if they rupture, your lungs flood with coolant and freeze harder than rock. Anyway, sweet dreams. See you in a year." Matt couldn't help but like him after that first encounter. They'd been tight ever since.

Matt slung Gatehouse's rifle and his supply bag over his shoulder, clipped off another smoke grenade, and tossed it outside. He waited a few seconds for another stray shot to smack into the hull and then leaped over the rim of the cabin.

Pinehurst watched him vanish into the hazy cloud of billowing smoke, sprinting for cover towards the base of some rocky cliffs. "Watch your six out there, brother," he muttered to himself, barely above a whisper.

FIVE

MATT STAYED LOW, moving up the steep and uneven terrain, pushing to acquire a good vantage point of the valley. Despite every slow and well-plotted step and the extra pounds of gear he was carrying, he was surprisingly agile.

That was until he stepped on some loose rock.

It sheared like slate, pitching him over, causing his stance to buckle. He began to slide back down the way he came, only to snag his other foot on a narrow ledge, breaking his descent.

Matt gave himself a moment to recover, his chest heaving hard. The sharp drop to the surface below was more than enough to shatter bones. He took in a few deeper breaths, swiping a small *water drop* icon that hovered above his forearm console. A clear fluid tube appeared inside his helmet, snaking up until it found his parched mouth. Matt feverishly sucked down some electrolytes, scanning the area, making sure he was nowhere near the vicinity of a Hellsting nest, which were always hard to spot.

Like some abominable cross between a coconut crab and an Emperor scorpion, Hellstings were fond of a booby-trap mechanism similar to that of the Australian trapdoor spider - utilizing an ultrathin membrane of silky material that stretched around the perimeter of their nests in a circular formation, acting as a tripline. It is common for wandering fauna to be completely unaware they have breached a nest until it's too late. If Matt was unlucky enough to trip a nest, or worse, fall into one, it would almost certainly mean death as they are extremely aggressive and territorial creatures.

With no eyes, these creatures hunt via a rim of hackles that form the dorsal crest of their heads. These are in constant motion, rippling in response to electromagnetic feedback humans are blind to. The average female is no larger than a full-grown alligator, but the needle-like stinger that protrudes from their bloated abdomens can easily puncture tank armor.

In addition to their deadly stingers, they also produce a highly toxic and corrosive venom called *Crystalline Vitelloxide*, which can be spat at prey from up to twenty meters away. A single drop is more than enough to kill a person if ingested or absorbed through the skin. In the previous year alone, several troops on ground patrols had met their demise this way. A constant hazard to both the USC and the Wraith, Hellstings were not to be trifled with.

Matt retracted his fluid tube and crested a rocky ledge until he reached a promontory that served as a good observational spot. He dropped to his knees, going prone on his stomach as he inched up to the lip of the slope. His HUD lit up, switching to the thermal binocular app which began automatically scanning and mapping the valley rift before him.

Matt took note of the scorching hot wind that whistled eerily between rocky crevices, and the low sun that hung like a blood clot in the sky, casting bizarre shadows, making this terrain feel even more desolate and alien.

He wheeled to his left, locating Darkhorse's crash site in the distance. The actual wreckage was obscured, but columns of smoke could still be seen pluming into the sky. Scavs circled way above, riding the unseen thermals that rippled between Epsilon's noxious clouds.

He turned to his right side and inched up some more to zero in on a cluster of rocky ledges that jutted out from an adjacent cliff face.

And that's when he saw it.

A spectral flutter of cloth stretched across the mouth of a small cave.

Matt slid the rifle off his shoulder, raising the scope to his eye. "Warhammer, this is Stryker actual. I have eyes on a possible HVT position. Grid forty-four, bearing two-two-seven-three-seven-four. How copy?" Matt's audio feed was met with a shrill of garbled static, causing him to wince. "Awesome," he muttered. "This day just keeps getting better." His eyes narrowed as his augmented binoculars zoomed in tighter on the point of interest.

The cloth was ragged and torn, shimmering in and out of his HUDs thermal spectrum, flapping loosely in the wind. There was no doubting it was Wraith tech. This was the target his scope had picked up earlier, which meant either Pinehurst was right, and this was a decoy, with the sniper's real location yet to be revealed. Or, Matt had located the sniper's nest and he was holed up somewhere inside. But first, he needed to investigate the Darkhorse crash site and check for any survivors.

Matt laid there for another twenty minutes, still as possible, his breaths shallow, eyes locked on the strange material. The sun was getting lower, but it was still hot enough to beat against his armor, threatening to bake him like a turkey inside an oven.

He lifted his faceplate and sifted some dirt through his armored fingers, bringing a clump up to his nose for inspection. He searched for a smell - something familiar - a faint trace-scent that might help conjure a memory of the planet he longed to return home to.

There was nothing. The dirt stunk of sulfur.

With no additional movement from the cave and no further shots taken at him, Matt was confident the sniper, wherever located, had not seen him escape their dropship wreckage. It was time to make his way over to the Darkhorse crash site.

Matt lowered his head and began to inch back down the slope, when he suddenly felt the surface beneath him shudder like a minor earthquake tremor. He immediately knew he was in trouble.

Deep trouble.

Before he could react, a full-grown Hellsting burst through a layer of fine shoal next to him, its hideous translucent stinger already poised to strike, glistening in the low sun.

"Ah, shit!" Matt cursed to himself. He'd been laying right next to a nest the entire time. He leapt to his feet as the Hellsting let out a bubbling hiss and scuttled towards him like some malformed spider.

Matt skillfully dodged a flurry of stinger blows, careful not to slip. He could feel the grip underneath his boots loosening against the rubble. One wrong move and he was a goner.

Now the Hellsting flicked its stinger around in the opposite direction, cracking it like a bullwhip.

Matt ducked under the lashes and unloaded a barrage of shots, firing from the hip.

The rounds pounded the upper shell, shattering it like brittle chips of bone. But the gunfire was hardly enough to stop its advance. The creature reared up like some rabid stallion, beating the air with its three pincers.

Matt had studied Hellsting behavioral patterns enough to know this gesture was a prelude to a *death-strike*, where the creature would dislocate the base of the stinger from its abdomen in order to extend its reach. It was an ideal maneuver for skewering larger prey while keeping a safe distance.

Matt also knew when the creature was poised like that, it revealed an inherent weak spot. He wasted no time firing at its exposed belly.

The Hellsting screeched in pain as fountains of milky-white blood erupted from its wounds, splashing over the rocky slope. It was gravely wounded, but Matt's actions made the god-awful thing even more pissed. The hackles across its back stiffened as it dropped low and started to circle him, now knowing better than to idle in his direct line of fire.

Matt could see it was losing a significant amount of blood. A single headshot would be enough to put it down. He raised the rifle to his eye, the scope reticles automatically locking onto the frontal lobe of its bulbous forehead. "Sayonara," he whispered before pulling the trigger.

Click... click-click-click!

Out of ammo.

Matt paled. "Oh, come on!"

As if sensing Matt's dilemma, the creature retracted two fleshy jowls around its gaping maw, unsheathing a long appendage like a mosquito's proboscis. Matt knew it was preparing to spit venom at him. If a single drop made contact, it would be the grand finale' to an already horrendously shitty day.

Never taking his eyes off the Hellsting, Matt ejected the spent ammo cartridge with lightning speed. Expert hands at work.

The empty cartridge clattered across the rocky surface, the residual effects of the high-capacity pulse rounds making it glow neon-blue.

Matt clipped a fresh cartridge off his belt and smacked it into the underside of the rifle. The second he heard the cartridge click into place, the Hellsting fired venom at him. It looked like a stream of cloudy water.

Matt leaped out of the way as it shot past him, torquing hard into a somersault. He broke the roll with his right knee. It was messy form, even reckless, but he needed to gain some distance before it could fire another shot at him.

Instead, the Hellsting charged Matt in a full-frontal assault, its pincers snapping wildly.

No time to line up another headshot, Matt began firing from the hip again.

The Hellsting shrieked as the rounds pocked its shell.

Matt never stopped firing until the Hellsting smashed into him like a sledgehammer, hissing and thrashing in its final death spasm. They both tumbled down the slope in a blur of dust.

Matt reached his arm out and snagged the base of a spire, canceling the momentum of his fall to a sudden jolt, nearly ripping his shoulder from its socket. He yelped in pain as the Hellsting barreled over him and continued over the cliff, plummeting into a narrow fissure below. After a few seconds, he heard the creature hit the bottom with a meaty thud.

Matt laid there for what seemed like an eternity, desperately trying to put some air into his wracked lungs. Epsilon's dense atmosphere wasn't doing him any favors. He was bruised, battered, and covered in Hellsting blood, which stunk like a mix of vinegar and three-day-old roadkill.

Upon painfully hoisting himself upright, he realized his supply bag had gone over with the Hellsting. He looked down at his belt seeing only one ammo cartridge remaining.

Matt let out an exhausted sigh. "Fuck this planet."

SIX

PINEHURST HELPED Kapernock and Strack lift Hernandez out of her chair. She was out cold, snoring louder than a freight train. Kapernock had managed to sever the top half of the girder that was connected to an overhead beam, freeing her impaled leg.

They gently laid her down, wrapping her in a thermal-cooling blanket. Direct exposure to Epsilon's sun for more than a few hours without hydrating often resulted in heat-stroke. So aside from electrolytes, cooling blankets were standard issue on every mission.

"How're we gonna get it out?" asked Strack, studying the other severed half of the girder that still grotesquely protruded from her leg.

"I'll worry about that, Spot. You hold her leg for me," ordered Kapernock.

Strack held Hernandez' leg out straight, while Kapernock signaled for Pinehurst to take a hold of the girder with him. "Grab the bottom, I'll grab the top. We pull it out on my mark." He held the top half of the girder with both hands, counting down. "Three, two, one... pull!"

They both ripped the girder out in one clean upward yank.

Kapernock tossed it aside while Pinehurst got started on stabilizing her leg. Using his own knife, he strip-cut her fatigues, forming a crude circle around the exposed wound. Then, he injected a sterilized tissue-filler deep into the wound, which looked like putty. It stemmed the bleeding instantly. Finally, he applied the shrink-seal. As the film of glue-like substance hardened, the wound began to seal up by itself.

"Nice work, fellas," Strack said, earnestly sucking on his helmet's fluid tube. "She's gonna be pissed as hell when she wakes up and finds out Matt's gone."

Pinehurst looked at Strack, realizing something. "That sniper ain't firing on us anymore."

Strack grinned. "Knowing Matt, he probably took him out already. Might even be on his way back. We should see if we can locate him on our scans."

Kapernock shimmied over to a new position against the cabin wall. "By all means, go ahead. But no way am I gonna tempt fate and stick my head up over this cabin. That sniper could still be watch—"

"Quiet!" hissed Pinehurst, interrupting. "You hear that?"

The three of them sat there in a breathless hush, listening to the hot wind that whistled through the dropship wreckage, moaning like lost souls of the damned. Buckled girders rattled, shredded steel flapped.

"You're gettin' spooky, Pinehurst," grumbled Kapernock. "It's just the wind."

But it wasn't.

Pinehurst raised his hand, motioning for Kapernock to be quiet. "Just listen."

In the far distance, something dark and hulking approached in the sky, looming into focus like some prehistoric flying monster.

Strack was the first to spot it. "I make one heavy inbound... definitely Wraith!"

The three of them grabbed Hernandez and quickly dragged her underneath a felled support beam.

Kapernock kept his eyes on the incoming ship, his jaw set firm. "Kill your heat-sigs!"

They each tapped a button on their forearm consoles, their armored suits shimmering before shutting down. Pinehurst reached over and killed Hernandez' suit. No HUD, no holographic icons or readouts, anything electronic was dead. If the approaching Wraith ship scanned the wreckage for any signs of life, nothing would show. If the ship decided to land, that would be an entirely different matter. But for now, the three of them remained hidden.

The ship dipped low and came in hard and fast; shovel-nosed, spiked with antennae, no windows, no wheels, and the unmistakable signature of Wraith propulsion technology - a low, rattlesnaking chatter from its unseen engines. Minutes felt like hours as it idled over the wreckage.

Then, the underside split open and the craft emitted a blinding white beam of light that began to probe the wreckage, forming a wide cone once it landed on the corpses of Gatehouse and Florez. There was a brilliant flash and the two bodies were gone. Vanished in the blink of an eye. The light went off and the ship ascended into the sky.

Kapernock and Strack sat there, staring with clouded disbelief as they watched the ship rapidly disappear over the horizon.

"What... what the fuck was that?" Strack whispered in a shaky voice, unable to take his dumbstruck eyes off the two vacant troop seats. "They just took Florez and Gatehouse. Just took 'em... some type of tractor beam or something." He wheeled to Pinehurst. "What was that, man?"

Pinehurst had no words. He'd only just remembered how to breathe again. "I don't know. But Hatchett said they've been stealing our dead, and we just caught a glimpse of how they do it."

"Stealing our dead? Worse than the fucking Scavs flyin' around out here," growled Kapernock, crawling out from his position. "These bastards won't even allow us the dignity of burying our fallen warriors!"

Pinehurst turned on his armored-suit and brought up the Darkhorse crash site location marker on his faceplate's HUD. That ship was headed in the same direction.

It was also the same direction Matt had gone.

SEVEN

THE DARKHORSE DROPSHIP wreckage was still smoldering by the time Matt reached it.

The troop cabin was nothing more than a charred shell, the sheared steel giving the appearance it had been raked by some giant set of talons.

The burned-out husks of dead soldiers littered the wreckage. Some had fallen to the surface like missiles, their crushed bodies rendered into shapes that barely resembled human form. Everything had been burnt to a cinder. There was nothing left to salvage.

Matt moved between the flaming piles of debris that were strewn throughout the site. He stopped at one blackened body, discerning what was left of the uniform. It was their pilot. He then lifted his faceplate to survey the sprawl of carnage, a windstorm of dust immediately netting in his eyelashes.

In the distance, he spied a large convex shape that had been torn open. It was a chunk of the cockpit. The pilot had been flung from it, landing where Matt now stood.

He lowered his faceplate again, and went to continue on when he heard a faint groan from somewhere behind him. He spun around to locate the source.

The body was a fair distance away, but Matt could clearly see it was a young male soldier, perhaps no older than twenty. Sections of his armored suit were cracked open, exposing charred and bloody flesh.

Matt rushed over to him, noting the rank decal and insignia on his armor. He was a private from Darkhorse Battalion's Indonesian regiment, *Tentara Nasional*, and he was in bad shape. His faceplate had been struck by something blunt and heavy at a very high velocity. The right side of his face was a sunken mash of shattered acrylic and bone. His right eye socket was nothing but a pulpy cavity. Both his legs were also pinned under a large support girder that had been torn from its bracket.

"Don't— don't leave me— please..." His voice was weak and pinched with fear.

Matt figured he didn't have long. Minutes at best. He had to do something. "I'm gonna get you out. Just hold on, private. That's an order!"

Matt scrambled over to the large girder, wedged his fingers underneath and began to lift it. It was heavy. Too heavy. The girder thudded back down to the ground. He took a deep breath and repositioned himself, squatting like a weightlifter about to perform a deadlift. This time, the girder began to rise, revealing the soldier's legs to be nothing more than flattened meat. Matt's own legs began to buckle. He growled with every ounce of strength he had, his face turning beetroot red, but he could not lift it any higher. It slammed back down on top of what remained of the soldier's legs.

He frantically looked around for something he could use to jam underneath the girder - something strong enough to keep it elevated while he dragged the soldier out.

There was nothing.

Matt turned and met the soldier's vacant eye. It was fixed on him in a *forever stare;* the look a soldier got when they knew the inevitable was near. There was no way Matt was going to be able to save this kid. All he could do was try and comfort him. He took a knee by the young soldier's side and grabbed his hand, holding it tight. "It's OK. I'm with you."

The soldier managed to give a tiny smile at that hint of reassurance.

"Where are you from?" Matt asked.

"Ban... Bandung," he said, his voice barely registering above a hoarse whisper.

"Where's that?"

"Small town... west... of Java."

"I bet it's beautiful."

The soldier nodded slowly, blinking sleepily.

"Think of it. Focus on your family and loved ones there. Let them take you home."

The soldier's gaze began to soften, drifting away from Matt, cast toward a future only he could see. His body gave one final tremble, his breath spluttering in shallow gasps. Then, he went still.

Matt let go of the limp hand and dropped his head. "They're gonna pay for what they did to us today," he whispered to himself. As he grabbed his rifle and stood, he paused, hearing something carrying with the wind.

Something unnatural.

It was the unmistakable rattlesnake chatter of a Wraith ship.

Matt took off like a rocket, sprinting across the crash site and diving behind a cluster of rocky spires. One of the spires was partially eroded and had formed a narrow fissure at its base. It was just wide enough for Matt to fit into, so he scurried over to it, rolled onto his back and wiggled inside. He then killed all the outputs on his suit, helmet, and weapon.

The Wraith ship slowed its approach, prowling low over the wreckage, kicking up a swirling torrent of smoke and dust in its wake.

Matt knew it had come from the direction of his own dropship crash site. He hoped what remained of his team had managed to evade capture, or worse.

The ship emitted its energy beam. It was so powerfully bright, Matt was forced to cover his eyes with both hands. Through his armored fingers, he was just able to make out clumps of wreckage debris levitating off the ground, rising up towards the belly of the ship. It took another few seconds for Matt to realize the beam was actually not sucking up debris, but the bodies of soldiers.

The ship continued to move through the wreckage in a strange stop-start motion, pausing to take each individual body. Some of the remains were nothing more than sloppy clumps of tissue and bone, yet the beam of light was indiscriminate about its choices. It was taking everything.

Matt watched in horror as the young private he had just comforted began to rise off the ground, the girder floating aside like it weighed no more than a feathered pillow. He felt a sudden urge to rush out and grab the soldier's arms before the ship took him, but thought better of it.

Once the ship was finished with its yield, the beam vanished and the ship rapidly ascended, streaking off into the sky. Within seconds, it had become a tiny glint against the ruddy sun.

Matt shimmied out from his hiding spot, turning his suit and rifle back on. He put the scope to his eye and managed to get a lock on the ship, tracking its trajectory before it completely disappeared over the horizon. He then lowered his rifle and waited for his HUD to calculate the data for him. Turned out, the ship's estimated flightpath fell into the same area as the sniper's nest he had located earlier.

Matt stood there for another moment, chewing over the data that streamed across his faceplate. Despite being reassured this place was a dead zone, nothing but Hellstings and Scavs, he could only draw upon the conclusion there was a hidden Wraith base somewhere close by.

A base the USC's *all-seeing* reconnaissance drones and satellites had somehow failed to locate.

EIGHT

MATT MOVED up the steep incline at a brisk pace. Epsilon's fading sun was still casting grubby shadows over the surrounding cliff faces.

Upon spotting the ragged cloth fluttering in the wind, he raised his rifle and slowed down to approach the cave entrance.

The cloth material was refracting prisms of light, like beads of water reflecting its surroundings. It also seemed to be malfunctioning.

Matt wondered if that was on purpose. An attempt to draw attention to this area. Maybe this was part of some elaborate trap he was walking into. In fact, he was beginning to think it was a certainty. *Epsilon is no place for heroes*, he thought, remembering the first prep-talk he received from his CO, only hours after he arrived. *Heroes are always the first to die on this rock. Don't be a hero.*

Matt sighed to himself. He was about to be a hero.

Using his rifle muzzle, he carefully brushed the cloth aside and slipped through the craggy opening, his faceplate and rifle scope automatically adjusting to the dimmer light. After a few more steps, the rifle's torchlight flickered on, revealing the cave to be riddled with stalactites and stalagmites, looking like the inside of an angry dragon's mouth. Steamy, geothermal pools of black mud bubbled away, condensation clouding Matt's visibility as he whisked past them. He lifted his faceplate, armored fingers clacking against it as he breathed in the hot and scummy air.

He pushed deeper into the dark, the cave widening to a narrow tunnel with a circular fracture at the end of it.

As Matt drew closer, his torchlight revealed it was not a natural rock formation, but a hatch of some kind, like a small metallic iris. To the right of it was a small control panel.

Matt approached the panel, taking his hand off the angled forward grip of his rifle to touch what appeared to be some type of clamp mechanism.

But before he could touch it, the audio feed in his helmet crackled with a terrible screech that reverberated throughout the tunnel, nearly giving him a heart attack on the spot. Underneath all the garbled interference, he recognized Pinehurst's faint voice. He was relieved to hear it. He figured they were still holed up back at the wreckage and were attempting to warn him about the Wraith ship that had been prowling around. "Pinehurst, how copy?" Another burst of garbled static shrilled into his ear.

Matt waited for the audio feed to go silent again, then reached for the clamp and pushed it downward in one swift movement.

There was a deep rumbling from within the cave walls. He backed away from the hatch, hearing what sounded like heavy internal locks moving. A series of triangular slits started reclining into the wall like a diaphragm adjusting to a new aperture.

Rifle up, Matt stepped through the open hatch, entering a vast corridor of artificial design.

Wraith design.

His torchlight danced erratically over the metallic walls that seemed to be streaked with some type of grease or oil. Intricate conduits of wiring ran along each side, giving it the look of a maintenance shaft that had been bored out of solid rock.

He continued on, panning his torchlight up to the ceiling to illuminate massive columns and retaining structures. Matt could also hear a dull mechanical hum emanating from inside the walls. He felt his grip tightening around his rifle as he pressed on.

Where was this all leading to? he thought. *Nowhere good.*

A shadow suddenly flashed across his field of view. He fired once, the round punched into the opposite wall, dislodging some tiny rocks in the ceiling above, sprinkling down onto his helmet.

A shift from behind him. Heavy footsteps scraping dirt.

Before Matt had a chance to turn, he was blinded by a white-phosphor explosion. It lifted him clean off his feet, blowing him down the corridor.

He hit the rocky surface hard, dazzled and partly deafened, trying to shake away the pain. But by that time, the seven Wraith soldiers had already surrounded him.

Matt only caught fleeting glimpses of their black-boned helmets and bizarre exo-suits as they began to restrain him.

One soldier ripped the helmet off Matt's head and cracked him in the jaw with his fist. Still reeling from the explosion and unable to focus, Matt thrashed and kicked, howling for his life with every ounce of strength he had left.

But it was futile. There was too many of them.

The last thing Matt felt was a tranq round punching into the side of his neck.

Then, darkness engulfed him for the second time that day.

NINE

THE BEAUTIFUL YOUNG woman shimmered in her white gown, ethereal, like an angel. She was in her mid-twenties, with tussled red locks that flowed carelessly over her delicate shoulders. Her brown eyes were warm and inviting. She chuckled, shaking her head with a mischievous grin. "Baby wake up. Come on, you're nearly home," she whispered, her voice, a discordant echo.

But she was met with silence. There was no response.

That worried her. The smile that played across her mouth vanished, her face twisting into a concerned glare.

Something was wrong...

TEN

MATT AWOKE, disorientated, unsure of where he was. As the last remnants of his dream began to fade, he suddenly remembered the ambush. His nostrils still stung from the hot discharge of chemical smoke, and there was also a foul acidic taste at the back of his throat, which he assumed was the narcotic agent they had used to subdue him. He had no idea how long he'd been unconscious for.

Realizing he'd been stripped of his armor and weapons, he lifted his groggy head, taking in the dank and clammy surroundings.

It was a small, honeycombed cell of some kind.

A sudden shift behind him caused him to sit up and turn. He was not alone in here. Another figure churned in the rank shadows.

"Hello?" Matt said, still trying to focus his eyes.

"Keep your voice down," the figure replied with a low snarl.

The other prisoner clearly sounded female. Matt couldn't exactly pin her accent, because oddly, she seemed to lack one. Instead, it sounded as if each word had been carefully curated before being spoken. Despite the dry croak in her throat, there was an elegance to her voice Matt had never heard before.

As his eyes adjusted to the low light, he could see the woman was a fellow USC officer. She wore similar fatigues to him, but they were more ragged and filthy. She was late-twenties, with raven hair and fair skin. Her blue-eyes seared with an authoritative disposition, and her features were sharp and well defined.

Matt also spotted a myriad of tiny puncture wounds around her neck and on her hands. He suspected those wounds were the result of a horrific torture technique the Wraith employed called *'Enhancement'*, where a series of long wires and needles were inserted into the victim's body, somehow increasing the sensitivity of the entire nervous system. This allowed incredible amounts of pain to be inflicted over long periods of time, without the subject ever falling unconscious or dying.

"What's your unit?" Matt asked in a softer voice.

"Kilo Company," she replied. "Master Corporal Adara Hughes."

"You're a combat engineer?"

"Third Battalion. *Draig Wen*."

"The White Dragons," Matt said with a respectful gleam in his eyes. "Better Death Than Dishonor."

Adara nodded. "That's us."

"Sergeant First Class Matthew Reeves. Black Skulls."

"Oh, a Praetorian. So was our overwatch," she replied with a cynical sniff. "They were the first to be taken out."

"I know," Matt said, wincing as he lifted himself to his feet. "That's why we came out here with Darkhorse - our op was to look for any survivors. We didn't get very far. Both our dropships were shot down."

"Well, you did manage to locate one of us," Adara said, pointing to herself with a wry grin.

"Is there anyone from Kilo left, aside from yourself?"

"There was ten of us, now there's three. At least that's how many screams I counted yesterday. The rest of the prisoners have all been shipped off."

"To where?"

"Someplace a lot worse than this, I imagine."

Matt looked up at the grimy ceiling, studying the tangled array of pipes that seemed to lead into an adjacent cell. His gaze then drifted down to the honeycombed bars that surrounded them. He could see the thin slivers of electrified energy rippling between each bar. "What is this place?"

"I don't really know. Some sort of processing facility."

Matt's frown deepened. "So they're luring our ships into the area, shooting them down, and then bringing the bodies here, dead or alive."

"Now you're catching on, Praetorian. How many of your guys survived that crash?"

"Five, including myself."

"They're here too?"

Matt shook his head. "Not yet. Hopefully, it'll stay that way."

"They'll be sending out retrieval ships."

"I know, I've already encountered one."

"What about Darkhorse Battalion?"

"All KIA."

Adara slumped back against the cell wall and breathed a defeated sigh. "All this for a couple of echo-box arrays. I don't even know what the crypto-codes were."

Matt looked at her incredulously. "They sent you out to install an echo-array without giving you any codes?"

"They were going to be sent to us once we landed. They never came. Shit, with everything going on, I'm amazed they even got the install site coordinates right."

"HQ gave us the codes before we left, just in case we located any of the boxes."

"Do you remember what they were?"

Matt shrugged nonchalantly. "Nope. But I'm pretty certain they were standard."

Adara scoffed. "Wow. No idea how Hatchett is going to un-fuck this situation."

"Got that right. Your accent— you don't sound Welsh."

"My father was in military intelligence after the invasion, so I traveled around a lot. Lived all over the world... guess over time, I just lost the accent—"

Matt jolted when a klaxon interrupted them and began to pulse through the entire facility, causing him to cover his ears. The deafening sound was like a ball-peen hammer tapping against his skull. "What the hell is that?"

Adara stood. "They're about to flush the lines. I hope you're not thirsty because this is the only water they give us."

Suddenly, the ceiling pipes opened with an explosion of air, blasting putrid water and pipe-scum down into the cell.

Matt crouched in an effort to shield himself from being doused with stinking sludge.

Adara did the opposite. She tilted her head upwards, opening her mouth as wide as she could.

Matt looked on in horror as she drank. He could hear the parched wails of the other prisoners in opposite cells, desperately trying to gulp down whatever they could before the pipes closed up again.

Once the pipes shut off, Matt moved as close as he could to the cell bars without touching them, peering out to see a dark yawning chamber, filled with strange equipment and supplies. He could make out several Wraith guards congregating around machines of war; enormous Arachnid-shaped tanks called *Stalkers*, and smaller, pod-shaped gunships dubbed *Death Ponies*. Beyond that - a big platform of some kind rumbled toward the ground, descending from an attached billet somewhere high above.

Matt's mind was churning furiously, trying to formulate some inkling of a plan. "I have to find a way to get out of this cell."

Adara gave a dry scoff. "You will soon enough when they come and take you for enhancement."

Matt turned to her with a grim look. "You got the wire?" he asked, dreading the answer he already knew.

"Three times now. So will you once they find out you were a Praetorian."

Matt was fucked. He dropped his head and sighed. "Just when I thought this goddamn day couldn't get any worse."

"You just have to take it. That's all you can do. The quicker you tell them whatever it is they want to know, the sooner it will be over. Don't be foolish like me."

Matt looked up at her inquisitively. "Why, what did you do?"

A small, but proud grin seeped into the corner of Adara's mouth. "I refused to tell them anything."

Matt mirrored her grin.

Adara's attention shifted to something behind Matt. She immediately rolled to her knees and bowed her head. "Get to your knees!" she hissed in a sotto voice.

As Matt spun to see what was behind him, the cell's honeycombed bars reclined back into themselves with a hard metallic snap.

Two Wraith guards stormed into the cell, their concrete-grey eyes gleaming from behind their hounskull-shaped helmets. Aside from their ghoulishly palid skin, the fact that they looked almost identical to humans made them seem even more terrifying. One of them barked at Matt in their native tongue, which to the human ear sounded like a rapid-fire staccato of clicks and snorts. Matt knew they were ordering him to kneel, so he obeyed.

At least, he made it appear that way.

He kept his eyes down, squatting, but making sure his knees never touched the ground. He would die before kneeling to a Wraith.

The two guards communicated with each other through violent bursts of their language as a gleaming black device hovered into the cell, passing between them.

Matt could hear Adara breathing like a racehorse. His eyes trained on a small puddle of sludgy water, which only offered tantalizing reflections of this strange machine. Then, Matt screamed as a burst of hot pain shot through his entire body. The device was a yoke. It collared his neck and fastened his wrists and ankles, then jolted him up upright into a sickening crucifixion pose.

One of the guards snorted with amusement at Matt's visible pain.

The other extended a cable with an articulated end that snaked through the air, searching for the matching cable on the top of Matt's yoke.

Once connected, the guards dog-walked him out of the cell, the bars snapping back into place behind them.

ELEVEN

MATT CRAB-STEPPED through the cavernous facility, passing towering pylons that crackled with strange energy. He figured this place had to be several stories underground from the planet's surface. Perhaps even deeper.

The two guards; leash holder in front, the other behind, began to lead him past the other cells. Matt was unable to turn his head, but his eyes pushed sideways, catching murky glimpses of USC prisoners inside their cells.

Some mustered the strength to raise their heads and meet his passing gaze, most did not. Adara believed only three POWs from Kilo Company were still detained here, but she was wrong. From what Matt could see, there were at least six, possibly seven.

With another shock of pain surging through his bones, Matt was abruptly halted.

The leash holder punched an old rusty control panel that looked like it had been Jerry-rigged with newer Wraith tech.

There was a harsh blatting sound, followed by a deep crack as the platform above detached from its billet.

Pain still lingering throughout his body, Matt did his best to look up, watching it descend towards him. As it drew closer, he could see another two guards riding the platform down, their imposing silhouettes set against the gloomy light.

The platform slammed into the ground with grim finality, and the guard behind Matt barked at him, nudging him in the back with the muzzle of his fist-gun. Matt awkwardly stepped onto the platform.

The platform docked with another heavy thud. Matt had mentally tracked his ascent, roughly calculating the platform was positioned at least three-hundred feet over the facility, give or take. One of the guards nudged him forward.

Still yoked, he was led off the platform towards a large triangular billet that looked to be carved straight from black marble. There was no visible windows or doors on the structure, just a strange purple gas that seeped from ribbed fissures around its underside.

When Matt and the guards reached the structure, a door flytrapped open in the middle, and another imposing Wraith guard greeted them.

This one was a Viscount guard. Its armor was way more grandiose and regal. The towering helmet was a circular crest of interlocking black spikes, reminding Matt of a peacock in full plumage. The Viscount snatched Matt's yoke leash and jerked it forward. As Matt stumbled through, the two other guards turned and marched off. The door snapped shut behind them.

The Viscount marched Matt into a small circular chamber, where two more Viscount guards stood.

But they were the least of Matt's concern.

There was an insidious-looking chair perched in the middle of the chamber. A chair Matt knew he was about to be forced to sit in. It bristled with needle-sharp spikes and a tangle of barbed-wires, looking like some type of alien Iron Maiden.

Matt could feel his heart thumping and the blood draining from his face simultaneously. He wanted to flee, heck, even stay and fight these guards, but he couldn't. He remembered what Adara told him.

You just have to take what they give you.

An energy pulse suddenly fired down Matt's leash, cracking open his yoke. It hit the ground with a heavy clunk, Matt's arms dropping to his side, limp as a rag-doll. For a split-second he was free, but before he could even consider acting on any impulses he may have had, he was hoisted up into the chair by the guards.

He immediately felt the chair's needled clamps snap around his neck, wrists, and ankles, sinking into his flesh. He felt paralyzed as some type of ice-cold substance began to course deeply through his muscles. The pain was unbearable.

Matt did what any person would do in this situation. He screamed.

TWELVE

MATT LANGUISHED IN THE CHAIR, the excruciating pain making him weaker by the second. He had no idea how long he'd been here, but he had the feeling the main event was yet to begin. His bloodshot eyes drifted around the room.

Artificial light from some unknown source skimmed the chamber walls, highlighting elements of what appeared to be a monochromatic relief. It was not art, more like a testament to the Wraith's existence. The relief featured a Wraith soldier, emblematic of their military theology and culture, standing tall and proud like an apex predator, surrounded by towering machines of war. There was a planet sitting underneath the Wraith's foot, which Matt assumed was Earth. The soldier's face was upturned towards the heavens, pondering which world to conquer next.

As Matt stared at the relief, something began to bubble up inside him. Something he immediately recognized as anger. It cut through the pain, sharpening his thoughts to a laser-thin focus. If he was going to survive and escape this facility, he needed something to cling to. This was it. No way was he done fighting yet.

You just have to take what they give you.

Suddenly, there was a low seething that began to surround him. It was as if the room itself was preparing for something, taking on a new wash of grim light.

"Most humans would still be screaming by this stage," said a well-articulated male voice from somewhere behind. "You must be special."

Matt grew increasingly baffled. *Was this another human prisoner sent up to interrogate me,* he thought. "Who are you?" he croaked, his throat drier than a pit of hot sand.

Footsteps approached. Matt saw the Viscount guards bow as a shadow passed them. Even though their postures showed respect, their eyes showed something else.

Fear.

Then, a male Wraith stood before Matt. He appeared older and taller - much thinner than the others he had glimpsed. His hollow grey eyes were fixed into a violating glare, and his ghastly features were more drawn and pronounced. The ceremonial armor he wore was befitting of a high-ranking officer. Matt instantly pegged him as the commander of this facility.

"You can speak English?" Matt said, failing to hide his surprise.

The Wraith smirked. "We are fluent in every language and dialect of the human race. We knew how to speak the English language before we entered your system."

Matt turned away from his interrogator. "Good for you. The stuffy Brit routine suits you well."

"The name you will address me by is Cromwell," he said in an overtly pompous tone. "I am your administrator. You have been selected for enhancement."

There was no reaction from Matt. His attention was trained on the wall relief opposite them.

That annoyed Cromwell. He turned to face it. "A glorious depiction, don't you think?"

"I'm guessing you had it carved before you decided to invade us."

Cromwell gave something that resembled a chuckle. "Ah, yes,

you humans are still under the impression that our retreat from Earth was your crowning moment of victory."

Matt's eyes shifted to the Viscount guards.

They had moved closer to him, their ornate fist-guns glinting in the dank light. Each guard also had some type of baton attached to their belts, like an electric cattle-prod.

He made a mental note of that, then decided it was time to get this show on the road. "Here's a little cheat sheet for you grey-eyed bastards - if you're going to invade a planet, perhaps figure out whether or not your technology will be affected by its magnetic field first."

Cromwell began to calmly circle the room. "Oh, I can assure you, the Combine has rectified that mistake."

"Really? Because last time I checked, we'd stolen a heap of your technology and used it to pursue you back here."

Cromwell paused to look at Matt, a malicious smirk spreading across his cadaver-pale lips. "And tell me, how is that working out for you?"

Point scored. Matt could only respond with a challenging glare.

Cromwell continued to circle the room as if he was on an afternoon stroll. "I wonder if it ever occurred to your military superiors that perhaps we allowed you to follow us back here. That perhaps we lured you to this planet on nothing more than a ruse..." Cromwell trailed off before meeting Matt's eyes again. "A ruse, no different from the myth we perpetrated to get *you* and your friends here."

Matt's breathing quickened upon realizing what Cromwell had just told him. *Was the Widowmaker nothing more than some kind of enemy psy-op the USC had fallen for?*

Cromwell stood there, waiting for a reaction from Matt to surface.

Matt did his best to maintain his poker face and brushed it off with a dismissive look. There was something about Cromwell's demeanor which Matt found unsettling. It went beyond a methodical manner. It bordered on the pathological.

Cromwell then moved in behind Matt. "No, you cannot even begin to fathom the plans I have for the human race," he said in a low and tense voice. He was close enough to Matt that he could smell the pungent stench of his breath.

Matt set his jaw firmly. "Look, if you're gonna torture and kill me, just get it over with."

"Enhancement is only for the purpose of conditioning. I have no intention of killing you... Matt."

Another flash of surprise rippled across Matt's eyes, which he failed to suppress.

Cromwell saw the reaction and smiled, his mouth splitting open like some cancerous wound, revealing mottled rows of phlegm-caked teeth. "You're wondering how I know your name. You think perhaps we managed to read the encrypted chip in your left hand. I can assure you, there was no need to do that. I already know who you are."

Matt swallowed his dry throat. "Well, in that case, would you mind if I leave?"

Cromwell snickered. "Your friends at the crash site will be dealt with soon enough. As for you - I'm not going to herd you off to another research facility like the other prisoners. Of course, once it was ascertained among the guards that you were a member of the fabled Praetorians, they wanted me to. But they don't see what I see. I see potential. I see an asset... Oh, no. I'm not here to take your life, Matt. I'm here to give it to you."

Matt glowered at him and scoffed. "You're trying to flip me? What makes you think I'd ever become a traitor to my own species?"

Cromwell leaned in even closer. "You are in a unique position not many humans will ever find themselves in. You are not even aware of it yet. The things you will see and do... The Combine have already sanctioned it, but regardless of their wishes, I am offering you to be part of something much bigger than the both of us."

Matt took a long beat before responding, feigning consideration.

"Wow, that's... that's quite the offer. But I'm going to politely decline and tell you to go fuck yourself."

Matt felt the chill from Cromwell's glare as he stepped away from the chair. "In that case, please allow me to show you exactly what it is we do here at this facility." Cromwell's eyes flicked to one of the guards.

Matt instantly felt the needles and wires sink deeper into his body, the pain stealing his breath away. There was a humming noise above as a thick shadow washed over him. He rolled his eyes upwards to see what was descending onto him.

It was a device that could only be described as a crown-of-barbs.

"Is this really necessary?" asked Matt, through clenched teeth.

Cromwell smiled at him. "No."

As the device pressed down over Matt's skull in a perverse coronation, an agonizing growl escaped his mouth. The barbs began to heat up, glowing as they bored through his flesh. Matt could not bear it any longer. He let out a gut-wrenching wail. This pain was unlike anything he'd ever experienced before. Every molecule and fiber in his body felt as if it were being torn apart. "Oh, Jesus! Stop it, stop it, stop it!"

Cromwell leaned closer again as Matt bucked and writhed in the chair. "I have plans for you, Matt. Such glorious plans."

THIRTEEN

NIGHTFALL HAD DESCENDED UPON EPSILON. The stars were barely visible through the murky atmosphere, casting them as faint smudges of sickly-colored light.

In the dropship wreckage, Pinehurst kept watch, scanning the valley at regular intervals with his HUD and rifle scope. He had grown increasingly irritated. He knew something was gravely wrong as there'd been no sign of Matt's return. It had also been hours since any sniper fire had rained down on their position. That pretty much stopped the moment Matt left the wreckage. He figured at this point, it was unlikely they'd see any support until sometime in the morning. That's assuming they could survive that long.

Kapernock and Strack were keeping an eye on Hernandez, monitoring her blood pressure and heart rate. They had synced up their helmet HUDs with the vital readouts on her armored suit. She had recently stirred awake and was re-hydrating with her electrolyte supply, although she was still groggy from the mammoth dose of morphine she had been given earlier. Her upper leg was heavily bandaged and now in a makeshift splint.

Strack had pulled the fluid tube from her helmet and reattached it to the bladder inside her armored suit, making it easier for her to replenish. She also kept herself wrapped in her thermal cooling blanket. Even at night, the planet offered little relief from the debilitating humidity.

Hernandez winced as she shifted her position, straightening her back against the cabin wall. "We got anything to eat?"

Strack reached for a supply bag and fished out a tin of food, handing it to her. "Bon Appétit."

Hernandez curled her lip while reading the description on the tin. "Teriyaki-flavored beef. Man, I'd give anything for a goddamn cheeseburger right now. You know this stuff is all freeze-dried on the trip out, right? It's not even real meat." She then peeled the tin open, pretending it smelled a lot better than it did and scooped out a clump with her fingers.

"I can't remember the last time I tasted real meat," pondered Kapernock. "Actually, I can't remember the last time I tasted real food. Now it's all that synthetically grown crap."

Strack watched Hernandez chew on her ration, grimacing at the taste. "I hope when we get back home we find out someone started up a new burger franchise. Or even one of the old chains, you know? One of the classics."

"Shit, at this point I'd settle for Dairy Queen," cackled Hernandez.

Strack and Kepernock chuckled in agreement, watching her struggle with a gristly piece of meat. After a few chews, she gave up and spat it out.

"Hey, any of you remember In-N-Out Burger?" asked Pinehurst, his eyes still glued to his rifle scope.

"Oh, dude, stop," said Strack, nearly salivating at the very thought. "I loved that place."

Hernandez' eyes lit up. "Hell yeah, I'm from California. I practically lived on Double-Doubles before the war."

"Their fries were pretty average, though," said Pinehurst. "The trick was to get 'em loaded, animal style."

"Never tried it. Any good?" asked Kapernock.

Hernandez and Strack looked at him dubiously, then at each other, unsure if Kapernock was just messing with them. "In-N-Out would've changed your life, bro. For real," said Hernandez.

Pinehurst nodded earnestly in agreement. "Ah, huh."

Kapernock leaned back against the cabin wall, his eyes drifting up to the night sky. "My dad used to tell me about this place he went to when he was a kid — four guys or something."

"Five Guys," quipped Pinehurst, his rifle still sweeping left-to-right over the lip of the cabin.

"Right. Anyway, he said they used to have this vanilla and bacon milkshake, said it was incredible."

"Vanilla and bacon? You're so full of shit, Kapernock," Hernandez huffed.

"Honestly, that's what he..." Kapernock's mouth went slack as he trailed off, spotting something approaching on his HUD.

Strack and Pinehurst's HUDs also began to blink red.

The object seared through the night sky, energy rippling from its rear. It was dark and sleek, like an ornate Medieval dagger.

Kapernock knew the shape all too well. "Wraith scout ship, incoming!"

At that moment, pulse rounds began to rain down on them like hellfire confetti. A large explosion fractured the rear of the cabin, throwing Pinehurst and Strack off their feet.

Hernandez wailed with pain as she lunged for the nearest rifle.

Kapernock ducked low under a felled support girder and started firing at the incoming vehicle in a futile blaze of glory.

His shots had little effect on the scout ship as it swooped low, unleashing another volley of fire on them. It then banked hard, twisting up into the night sky, disappearing over the rocky horizon.

Pinehurst crawled to his feet, bracing for another incoming burst of fire.

But it never came.

"Where's our goddamn QRF?" snarled Kapernock, covered in grit and debris, madder than a cut snake.

"It's gone!" yelled Strack, helping Hernandez back upright.

"No shit, Captain Obvious," snapped Kapernock, brushing away the dirt that now caked the neckline of his armored suit.

Pinehurst looked in each direction, his ears radar dishes. He turned and caught Hernandez watching him.

She knew exactly what Pinehurst was thinking. The ship was indeed gone, but the threat wasn't. "Something tells me they were just softening us up," she said.

That's when their HUDs began flashing in unison again, picking up a fresh batch of incoming targets.

Pinehurst, Kapernock, and Strack hustled to the edge of the cabin, rifles up to their eyes as they trained them on the pitch-black valley.

"We got incoming! Ten o'clock!" yelled Kapernock.

Within seconds they got a lock on a dozen shapes moving towards their position.

"Ground targets are one-hundred yards out and closing. I count twelve. Confirm!" barked Pinehurst.

"Confirmed," said Strack.

"Confirmed," said Kapernock. "Twelve incoming fast!"

"Get me on my feet," grunted Hernandez, slipping her helmet over her head. "I can't do shit down here."

"Strack, get her up," ordered Pinehurst. "Quickly!"

Strack broke position, bending down to loop Hernandez' arm over his shoulder. Once on her good leg, Hernandez hopped over and took position between Pinehurst and Kapernock, with Strack repositioning on their right-side.

Hernandez quickly adjusted the settings on her rifle scope, reticles flashing as they recalculated a new distance. She then put the scope to her faceplate, leaning her weight forward against the cabin.

"They just cloaked!" said Kapernock. "Can't see them in my scope anymore."

"Talk to me. What're you thinkin', fellas?" Hernandez whispered tensely, ready for war.

"I'm thinking we're about to get into a pretty good gunfight," replied Kapernock.

"They're still out there. Switch thermals," ordered Pinehurst.

The four of them tapped the side of their helmet. The second their HUD scans switched to another light spectrum, their faceplates lit up, highlighting multiple targets. And there was way more than a dozen infantry.

There was fifty.

"Oh... shit! Ah— I now count fifty targets and closing!" yelled Hernandez.

Through their scopes, dozens of globular shapes began to form over the ridge of the valley floor, grey eyes glinting in the dark like a pack of wild predators.

"Light 'em up!" barked Pinehurst.

The four of them began firing, the crackle of their gunfire pinballing off the surrounding cliff faces.

The Wraith returned fire, jacketed pulse rounds lighting up the valley floor in brilliant hues of blue.

All hell had broken loose.

FOURTEEN

ADARA STOOD by the honeycombed bars in her cell, watching the platform dock. She was expecting to see Matt near-comatose like so many of the other prisoners who returned from enhancement. Some ended up so weak and frail, the guards literally had to drag them back to their cells.

But to her surprise, Matt was still on his feet. From what she could make out, there was the usual accompaniment of two guards, one holding the leash attached to his yoke, the other standing at the rear. It was clear he was struggling to stay upright, but he was walking.

Adara moved away from the bars and sat in the corner of the cell. Whoever this soldier was, he was stronger than any of the other prisoners here. But she also knew every human had their limit, and the Wraith would continue their enhancement until he gave them what they wanted - which was nothing less than complete submission.

The cell doors snapped up with a harsh clang. The guards hustled Matt inside.

Close up, he looked a lot worse than she had initially thought. He was dipping in-and-out of consciousness, the fresh enhancement wounds riddled around his neck and up his arms were still bleeding.

The guards unyoked him. He collapsed into a heap on the ground.

As Adara watched the guards turn and march out of the cell, she figured it would take another day or two, maybe three at best before they broke him.

FIFTEEN

MATT WAS STILL flat on his back when he came to. His entire body was reeling with crippling pain. His breaths were short, shallow gulps, and his face was a pale mask of beaded sweat. The enhancement wounds riddled over his body still throbbed like hell, making him feel like a human pin-cushion.

"The best thing you can do is just lay there, still as possible," Adara said. "The pain will ease a little by the morning. Unfortunately, that's also when they'll come for you again."

Matt's lips parted. Nothing came out except a hollow sigh. He tried again, barely able to form the words. "Call... the... call the guards."

Adara looked at him like he was a lunatic. "You're delirious, try not to speak."

"...Call them..."

"You don't know what you're saying?"

"Just— call them. I need help."

Adara kept her glare on him and scoffed. "You think the guards are going to help you?"

"Please..."

Adara moved over to the bars of the cell and gingerly peered out. "Hello?" Her voice echoed throughout the block, but it was only met with stale silence.

"Try again."

She turned around to Matt. "Seriously, are you trying to get us both killed?"

Matt laid there on his back, his eyes studying the rancid ceiling pipes that still dripped putrid water. "Please— try again." He rolled over onto his knees, struggling through the pain.

Adara watched him curiously. Maybe he really did need help. "Guards! I need help over here," she yelled even louder. "Help! We need some help in here!"

The entire base seemed deserted. Then, two guards appeared from the murky shadows.

Adara recoiled, backing away from the cell door as it snapped up.

The guards entered to see Matt on his knees, buckled over with his face down, his shoulders heaving uncontrollably. It appeared he was having some kind of seizure.

One of the guards looked up and spat an insult at Adara, pissed for being hailed over something as meaningless as a sick prisoner.

The other guard nudged Matt hard with the tip of his combat boot.

Matt remained there, back facing them, shuddering and whimpering softly.

The guard then ordered Matt to stand. When he did not obey, the guard drew a long cattle-prod from a belt-holster and went to strike him.

That's when Matt sprung to his feet with the speed of a panther and snatched the guard's arm, wrenching it forward.

The tip of the prod hit the other guard in the chest. Despite the armor plating of its exo-suit, the electric discharge was powerful enough to send him flying across the cell. He slammed hard into the opposite wall and collapsed into a heap on the ground.

Still holding the arm of the guard with the prod, Matt kicked his legs out in one clean motion, and before there was a chance to recover, twisted the arm inward so the guard stabbed himself with his own prod. The guard screamed as thousands of volts went postal through his body. Matt knew all this commotion would draw attention, so he had to act quickly while the cell doors were still up.

When the guard's body went slack, Matt dropped the crackling prod and reached for the holstered fist-gun. "Come on, let's get outta here!"

"Don't touch that weapon, Matt."

Matt spun around to see Adara already had the other guards fist-gun trained on him.

Matt paled. "The hell are you doing?"

"Cromwell anticipated you might try something like this," she said, stiffening her aim. The concern on her face from before had melted away. It was now replaced with an icy detachment.

She was a Wraith.

Matt could feel his fists tightening. While enhancement was for the purpose of turning human prisoners into Wraith spies, Matt also knew about *Infiltrators*; genetically grown Wraith operatives who looked and sounded identical to humans. The very notion that the Wraith could one day successfully mimic and penetrate USC high command was the kind of thing that kept people like Hatchett awake at night.

Adara grinned when she saw Matt's eyes harden from the realization of what she was. "I was tasked with comforting you. We thought something familiar would help." She stepped closer to him. "You can still leave this place, Matt. But only once you have completed your enhancement."

Everything around Matt seemed to narrow until there was nothing but the thunder of blood in his ears, and the echoed din of guards mobilizing throughout the base. Any moment, dozens of them would be in the cell subduing him in a yoke - or worse - another tranq round. "Yeah, like I told Cromwell earlier, I'm not in the market for a new job."

"He has plans for you, Matt. Such wonderful plans."

"How thoughtful of him."

"Our human assets are also expendable. Losing you would be nothing more than a minor inconvenience."

Matt saw her shift her stance. She was readying to line up a shot in case he tried anything.

One of the guards on the ground stirred, groaning in pain.

Adara took her eyes off Matt for a split-second.

That was all the time he needed.

Matt charged at her like a mad bull. His attack came in wild and clumsy, but the force of the impact was enough to send them both flying across the cell.

They hit the opposite wall, Adara grunting as air was expelled from her lungs like a blown tire. The two of them went down hard, crashing to the ground in an untidy heap of flailing limbs.

Matt wrestled with her gun arm. She was incredibly strong. He could also smell a stale odor from her that was similar to Cromwell. With both hands clasped firmly around her wrist, he began to bash her gun arm against the ground in a motion that looked like he was attempting to knead dough. Her hand spasmed and the fist-gun was gone, spinning across the floor of the cell.

Matt then brought his arm up and drove the elbow down onto her jaw. Her head rocked, but the blow was inadequate. She already had her free hand clutched around his throat. Hot chugs of breath gusted from her mouth as she began to apply pressure to his windpipe.

At that point, Matt started to hear everything through a filter of blunted sound. The color was draining from his vision as his eyes rolled back into his skull. He could feel consciousness leaving him. He tried to loosen her vice-like grip, but it was too powerful. When she felt his body relax and slump, mercifully, she released the pressure on his throat. He collapsed to the ground and Adara picked herself up, calmly walking over to the fallen fist-gun.

Dizzy and unfocused, Matt sat up, gulping for air like a fish out of water. He could see Adara gathering the gun in her hand. He could also just make out the other holstered fist-gun on the knocked-out guard. Mustering every last drop of strength he had left, he lunged for it, snatching the weapon out of its holster. He then scurried to his feet and broke into a half-assed sprint. As a parting gift, he pivoted around and fired a shot at Adara.

Adara yelped as the fist-gun bolt grazed the top of her shoulder, punching into the wall behind her. She returned the gesture, unloading a barrage of shots, but Matt was already long gone. She followed him out of the cell, screaming for the guards to assist.

A klaxon began to drone loudly from somewhere high above.

Fist-gun bolts strafed Matt as he slid for cover behind a row of hexagon-shaped supply containers.

Peering out between two stacks, he could see the nearest Death Pony was berthed about one-hundred meters away. Quite a sprint for someone still trying to breathe. Nevertheless, he needed to reach it before the guards did. If those coilguns got a lock on him, his escape attempt would be over quicker than it began. In a few seconds, the entire base would have him surrounded. He needed to get moving again.

He broke cover and fired another volley of shots at Adara, who was using the cell for cover, then took off towards the nearest Death Pony.

A few prisoners caught glimpses of Matt tearing past their cells and began to cheer him on.

Up ahead, Matt could see Wraith guards emerging from the darkness, closing in on him fast.

A bolt cracked into the ground before him, throwing up a geyser of grit into his eyes. He pitched forward but managed to stay upright on his feet. After another bolt cracked into a pylon, inches from his head, he started to run zig-zag, knowing Adara's impaired aim would eventually find its mark.

Matt reached the Death Pony and leaped onto its beetle-black hull.

The first guard to reach the craft also followed him up, cattle-prod poised to strike.

Matt swung around and fired at the guard. The bolt missed, so he stomped the guard in the chest with the heel of his boot. The blow rocked the guard backward, but as Matt went to retract his leg, the guard snatched it and jammed the prod into his calf muscle.

Matt screamed as the discharge crackled through his entire body. But he had felt worse pain that day. A lot worse. He leaned forward and unloaded his fist-gun again, this time scoring a direct headshot.

The guard tumbled off the side of the craft.

He turned and continued on with his climb, dropping down inside the pod-shaped cockpit.

The first thing he noticed was the lack of any seats. There was only a circular bracing platform for stand-up piloting. Secondly, the control dash underneath the holographic viewport was a Rubik's Cube of kinetic braille, rippling and seething, imparting all kinds of information Matt had no chance of using, let alone ever understanding.

He would have to wing it.

The only thing he could relate to were the two metallic horns that protruded out from the control dash. It had to be some type of steering device. With the muffled voices of the guards outside growing louder and more excited, Matt grabbed the horns and gave them a downward tug.

The craft lurched forward, smashing against its berth. Guards that were scrambling up the hull were suddenly flung off. A few standing in front of the craft were knocked over like bowling pins.

Matt saw a group of guards mounting the other Death Ponies. He yanked the horns to his left and the craft spun around to face them. He could feel two circular indents on each horn. He pressed them, and the craft began to spew javelins of molten-blue plasma from its coilguns, obliterating the other craft in a flash of fire and metal. He spied two more Death Ponies berthed at the very far end of the facility but destroying them was a luxury he did not have the time for. He spun the Death Pony around to face the row of occupied cells.

The prisoners standing by the bars, gleefully watching the chaos unfold, knew what he was about to do. They all scurried away, curling up into the corners of their cells.

Matt fired a single burst at each cell, shattering the honeycombed bars like rock candy.

The seven prisoners gingerly exited their cells, trading looks of disbelief with each other. They were all emaciated and half-dead, but upon spotting the unit of Wraith guards now rushing towards them, broke into a hard sprint, propelled by the only thing they had left - the will to survive.

Adara broke cover from her cell to see the seven prisoners escaping on foot. She began firing on them.

One prisoner was struck in the arm, spinning him like a bottle top. He fell hard and skidded across the ground on his stomach.

Two of the fleeing prisoners turned and ran back to help their fallen comrade, fist-gun bolts cleaving the air around them. They grabbed the wounded prisoner by the legs and started dragging him towards the Death Pony Matt was commandeering.

Matt saw that Adara was lining up another shot, so he swung the craft around to face her cell and opened fire.

The coilgun hammered her position, reducing the entire cell block to nothing more than a fiery crater. There was little chance she would have survived Matt's onslaught. That was perfectly fine by him.

Hearing some of the prisoners climbing up onto the hull, Matt let go of the horns and popped open the cockpit hatch. When he returned back to the control dash, he saw there were more guards riding the platform down from the overhead billet. Some of these guards looked to be manning heavy thermite cannons and rotary plasma launchers.

He needed to get this pony airborne.

One-by-one, the prisoners tumbled into the cockpit, some landing on their asses with a hard thud. The cockpit was not designed for more than two occupants, so it was already cramped and humid. The prisoners stunk like a mix of stale urine and wet dog. There were five men and two women, all from Kilo Company. The last one through reached up and sealed the cockpit.

Matt spun around and gave them an earnest nod.

They all returned it. Cradling his bleeding arm, the wounded prisoner started cackling like a Hyena, unable to accept the fact that he was still alive and being rescued.

"Hold on!" Matt yanked the steering horn down.

There was a deep rumble as the Death Pony dipped and then began to rise up towards the billet. Once Matt was level with the platform, he destroyed it with a few rattling bursts, causing the platform's spine to collapse. The guards plummeted into the smoldering heap of twisted metal below.

Flanked by his three Viscounts, Cromwell moved up the shuddering billet ramp to gain some elevation over the carnage, when the Death Pony shot past him, its coilguns blasting the sealed bay doors overhead, which looked like the glossy shell of some giant insect. Cromwell ordered the Viscounts to bring the craft down. They opened fire.

Suddenly, the Death Pony snapped around and returned fire. The three guards vanished in a cloud of pink mince, forcing Cromwell to rush back down to the opposite end of the ramp before Matt's coilguns severed it in half.

Matt thought he glimpsed Cromwell through the thick haze of smoke and fire, but breaking position to pursue him would only cost more precious time. He spun the pony back around and veered the craft closer to the bay doors. He began firing again on the same spot, the sound of his coilguns quickly morphing into a deafening thunderclap. Matt just needed to make a hole large enough to fly through.

Cromwell watched intently from the base of the shattered ramp, unable to do anything to stop them from escaping. The facility was severely damaged, and most of his Garrison had been turned to ash in a matter of minutes. The Combine would not be happy. There would be repercussions. But despite all of that, a smirk began to form across his cruel mouth. He knew this would not be the last time he ever saw Matt again.

The Death Pony punched through the hole of glowing slag and shot off into the night sky.

SIXTEEN

THE DEATH PONY broke through a stratus of boiling clouds.

"I'm goin' low," Matt barked over his shoulder.

The prisoners held on as Matt vectored the craft towards a dark ribbon of canyon. The wounded prisoner was still laughing, having the time of his life.

Matt couldn't help but crack a grin. He was actually starting to get the hang of the controls.

Thwap-Thwap-Thwap!

Pulse fire rocked the cockpit. Matt leveled out and yanked the horns. The pony spun around while still moving forward.

Two more Death Ponies were closing in on them.

Matt cursed himself for not taking care of them when he had the chance.

Holographic representations of the pursuing craft suddenly appeared above the control dash, rendered in strange three-dimensional biorhythms. Gently swirling around the imagery was a series of animated glyphs, which Matt assumed was some type of targeting apparatus. He tapped one and the cockpit began to pulse crimson-red, followed by the drone of multiple engines powering-down at once. Then, everything in the cockpit went completely dead. Nothing but the whistling sound of wind.

The prisoners traded looks. Except the wounded one. He was laughing even louder now.

Matt's brow creased. "Um... that can't be good."

He tapped the glyph again and the blinking stopped. The engines powered back up. But this time the holograph had disappeared over the dash.

"Shit," Matt huffed to himself. There was no time to figure all this out. He looked at the two ponies bearing down on them. He would have to use his naked eye for targeting. He pressed the indents on his steering horn and coilgun started belching blue fire.

Both ponies broke formation and banked hard out of Matt's line of fire. One of them dipped underneath his position, tilted itself upwards and fired.

Matt saw the maneuver and spun the ship, evading the burst of fire from below. He then revolved the pony around to face forward again and punched the throttle. The craft took off at an astonishing speed.

The two pony's gave chase.

Matt dropped into the canyon, threading his way through the narrow ruts of black rock.

Up ahead, canyon walls started exploding as Matt's pony was raked with more fire. Instead of trying to dodge the falling chunks of rock, he decided to punch through them. A wash of debris peppered the craft like heavy hail on the roof of a car.

Then, another alarm began flashing. This one was on the viewport display, warning Matt about the towering ridgeline he was approaching. He yanked the horns down and the pony shot up out of the canyon. Everyone except Matt was violently propelled to the back of the cockpit, mashed together in a tangle of limbs.

The wounded prisoner had finally stopped laughing.

Matt was done with this cat and mouse bullshit. He hit the brakes.

Both ponies overshot him.

Matt's control dash suddenly lit up like a Christmas tree. The holograph of the two ponies had not only reappeared, they were both tagged with flashing triangular icons. Matt knew it was the onboard targeting system indicating it had multiple lock-ons. After being fired upon, it had reclassified the other craft as enemy bogies. He exhaled and opened fire.

The coilguns lit up the night sky with rails of blue plasma. Both ponies were disintegrated in a giant cloud of electrified ash.

The prisoners began to cheer and whistle.

Matt felt like he was going to collapse with exhaustion. He turned to them with a tired smile.

SEVENTEEN

HERNANDEZ SPOTTED three Wraith infantry pushing towards their right side, using the deep-winding furrows of eroded rock as a natural form of cover. When they reappeared, they were close enough to see clearly. "Right flank! Right flank!" Hernandez yelled as she opened fire on them.

Pinehurst, Kapernock, and Strack pivoted and also began firing into the right flank.

One of the Wraith soldiers was hit, the other two leap-frogged into another furrow and disappeared again.

"Strack!" barked Pinehurst.

"Sir!"

"Keep suppressing that flank!"

"Roger that." Strack kept his weapon trained on the furrow the two Wraith soldiers were hiding in and continued firing.

As Strack's rounds punched into the top of the ridgeline, thick clumps of dirt and rock spewed into the air like a volcanic eruption.

Pinehurst, Kapernock, and Hernandez swung back around to fire at the wall of Wraith soldiers advancing on them.

Pinehurst's rifle started beeping, indicating he was about to run out of ammo. He dropped down behind cover to swap out his cartridge. "This is not good," he grunted to himself while fishing out a fresh cartridge, the barrel of his rifle glowing iridescent blue, hot enough to char cloth.

Then, Kapernock dropped down and joined him, swapping out his ammo cartridge. "Fuck me, they're coming outta the goddamn rocks. We can't hold this position, Mikey. We gotta bail."

Pinehurst smacked the new cartridge into the butt of his rifle. "And go where?"

"Any place but here."

Pinehurst shook his head, noticing he only had two cartridges left in his pouch. "With you and Strack carrying Hernandez, we wouldn't make it ten feet without getting mowed down."

"So what's our option? Stay *here* and get mowed down?"

Hernandez swiveled left and saw twenty more Wraith infantry coming up over a crest, moving into firing position. One of them was lifting something heavy onto its shoulder. It was akin to an RPG launcher. Hernandez saw it and paled. "Plasma javelin! Left side!"

There was a sharp crack as the javelin rippled through the air, hitting just short of Hernandez and Strack, blasting them backward. The force of the explosion was strong enough to rock the entire cabin.

Pinehurst and Kapernock jolted forward from the impact, then swung themselves up over the lip of the cabin and began firing into the left position.

The Wraith soldier holding the plasma launcher was torn to shreds before it could reload.

"Hernandez! Strack!" yelled Pinehurst in between bursts of return fire.

"Yeah," groaned Strack.

"You OK?"

Strack peeled himself off the ground, covered in dirt and rock. "We're good, sir," he said through mashed teeth.

Hernandez winced as Strack looped his neck under her right arm and hoisted her upright. "Ain't dying on this rock until I get my fucking cheeseburger," she said, lifting her faceplate to spit blood and snot.

Strack coughed out a dry laugh. "Amen to that."

Through the strobe-like flashes of blue gunfire that lit up the valley floor, Kapernock and Pinehurst could see more Wraith amassing on both sides, dialing in on their position. When the cabin was sprayed with another torrent of pulse fire, they were both forced to duck and take cover, incoming rounds tearing over their heads.

"Ammo count!" yelled Pinehurst.

Kapernock checked his rifle readout and his supply pouches. "Eighty rounds. One full cartridge."

"I've got two full cartridges and one grenade," replied Pinehurst.

Hernandez tossed her rifle down. "Sorry, fellas. I'm out."

Kapernock unholstered his side-arm and slid it over to her. "Make 'em count."

Hernandez grabbed the smart-targeting pistol and gave him an exhausted nod. "Thanks."

Strack looked down at the blinking ammo readout on his rifle. "Well, this all feels very unsurvivable. Fifty rounds."

Over the crackle of gunfire, they could hear the Wraith communicating with each other as they pressed closer, threatening to overwhelm them at any moment. Another hail of heavy fire slammed into the cabin, Wraith voices growing louder.

Hearing the voices, Kapernock closed his eyes and breathed deep. "I want every Praetorian to know we died taking on a hundred of these assholes. I want them to know I died fighting alongside my brothers and sisters."

"Fuck yeah, they'll know," said Hernandez. "But we ain't dead yet."

Suddenly, the Wraiths gunfire stopped, replaced by a deep rumbling.

The four of them shared tense looks as the cabin began to vibrate, the rumbling growing louder, strange mechanical sounds ricocheting off the walls of the valley.

Kapernock turned to Hernandez and gulped. "Yeah. We're dead now."

Pinehurst jumped up and gingerly peered over the lip of the cabin, sighting down his muzzle to locate the source of the rumbling.

A huge Stalker loomed into view as it clanked along the valley floor like some mechanized prehistoric spider, its treads crushing the rocky ground into puffs of dust. Riding the turret was a wispy-looking Wraith Commander. He was barking orders to the rows of infantry trailing behind him.

Pinehurst breathed a defeated sigh. "I see one heavy inbound… it's a Stalker."

Kapernock jumped up to join Pinehurst. "Jesus, haven't these guys ever heard of overkill? There's only four of us."

Strack and Hernandez both wearily leaned against the cabin. Strack took off his sweat-drenched helmet, dropping it into his lap. As the HUD readouts on his faceplate died, he looked up at Hernandez. "It's been an honor, Sergeant."

Hernandez gave him a respectful nod, then tilted her head to the angry red cloud bands that flecked the sky. Dawn was approaching. "Likewise, Commander Spot. Likewise."

Pinehurst and Kapernock still had their sights trained on the Stalker as it lurched towards them, clearing several feet with each step.

The Stalker's commander had dropped down into the turret and was now aiming the primary cannon directly at them. All remaining infantry shuffled in line behind the Stalker as the tip of its cannon began to glow white-hot, rippling with energy. It was powering up to fire on their position. One shot and the dropship cabin would be obliterated.

"Fuck it," snorted Pinehurst, as he opened fire on the Stalker.

The pulse rounds bounced off its black hull, a shower of blue sparks lighting up the humid air around it.

Knowing the futility, Kapernock also started pumping his trigger, but the Stalker kept advancing.

Strack helped Hernandez onto her feet. No way was she going to die sitting on her ass. They both lined up next to Pinehurst and Kapernock and started firing on the Stalker with whatever ammo they had left, their cartridges running down to the final rounds.

Thwap-Thwap-Thwap-BOOM!

Suddenly, the Stalker exploded into a massive fireball. Churning gouts of flame shot high into the sky as the infantry scattered like roaches. Another explosion sent the cannon turret spiraling into the air like a flaming pinwheel.

The four Black Skulls stared with amazement, their jaws slack as a Death Pony swooped down into the valley and eviscerated multiple clusters of Wraith infantry with its coilguns before rising up into a steep climb. It then came around for another pass, dropping low to line up its next wave of carnage. The remaining infantry began to retreat, some running aimlessly, others desperately trying to reach cover as coilguns pelted them into clouds of black ash. It turned and pulled into another steep climb, soaring into the pre-dawn sky.

Pinehurst stared up at it, unable to speak at first. "That's... guys, that's gotta be Matt."

"How do you know?" asked Kapernock, his eyes still tracking the enemy ship with caution.

"Because Matt's the only person I know crazy enough to attempt something like this."

Strack began laughing. Hernandez raised her pistol, whooping and hollering at the sky.

The surviving Wraith infantry raced off into the fleeting shadows, leaderless and confused.

EIGHTEEN

MATT BROUGHT the Death Pony back around to begin his landing descent.

It was at that moment he realized taking off, flying, and landing were three different scenarios. With no idea how this craft was supposed to land, he would have no choice but to force a crash landing as gently as possible without killing everyone inside, including himself. With a little luck, he'd have bragging rights on surviving two separate crashes in one day. He figured that had to be a record.

He pulled back on the throttle. "Sorry to do this to you again, but this might... hurt. Hold on."

The prisoners were getting used to this. They began to brace themselves for impact.

Matt could feel the steering horn vibrating hard as he dropped into the valley again, trying to control the craft as the ground rushed up to meet him. He leveled out the steering horn as much as he could, gliding a few feet above the surface to dampen the impact.

Then, the craft hit the ground. Everyone was violently flung forward. Sheared rock piled up over the viewport as the craft skimmed recklessly along the valley floor, plunging the cockpit into complete darkness. Finally, the Death Pony came to a grinding halt.

Hernandez stayed with the dropship wreckage, keeping her weapon trained on the downed enemy craft as Strack, Kapernock, and Pinehurst cautiously made their way out, their rifles sweeping over the ruins of dead Wraith infantry.

As they closed in and surrounded it, the cockpit hatch popped open, forcing them to freeze. Rifles up, they waited with bated breath to see what would appear.

When two human hands slowly emerged, the three of them breathed a collective sigh of relief.

Matt stuck his head up. "Got some soldiers here who need help. Mind giving me a hand?"

"Where's your helmet?" asked Strack.

"You sure you wanna know?" Matt said, a sly grin forming in the corner of his mouth.

Pinehurst laughed and shook his head. "Matt, you really are one crazy son of a bitch, you know that?"

NINETEEN

EPSILON'S SUN was yet to fully breach the horizon, but its morning heat was already baking the dropship wreckage.

Kapernock and Strack had tied-off both ends of a thermal cooling blanket, stretching it between two girders to form a makeshift tarpaulin cover. It would help shield the rescued prisoners from the sun's rays. Three of them were severely dehydrated. The other four were dangerously close, so weak they could barely sit upright.

"...Let me get this straight - you escaped an enhancement facility?" Hernandez said, still unable to believe what she had just heard.

Matt nodded while helping one of the soldiers from Kilo Company drink from an electrolyte flask.

"Not only escaped, but rescued seven of us and piloted that damn thing back here," the rescued soldier croaked.

Hernandez studied the riddle of pin-prick wounds on Matt's neck and hands, then turned and looked out at the partially submerged Death Pony resting lopsided on the valley floor. "They're gonna give you a medal for this, Matt."

Matt shrugged. "A cryo-pod back to Earth would suffice."

"Might need to worry about how we're gonna get back to base

first," said Pinehurst. "No way can we pilot that thing. We wouldn't make it within a hundred clicks of base before—"

KA-BOOOOM!

Everyone in the dropship cabin jolted from a massive explosion. It took them a few moments to realize the Death Pony was now a billowing fireball.

Matt looked up to see two USC *Wasps* descending on them, with a larger Destroyer class gunship circling overhead like a bird of prey, its plasma cannons glowing hot.

Wasps were the most agile attack choppers in the USC's inventory. Many military historians had compared them to the decommissioned *Blackhawks* that were used in the earlier part of the 21st century, except these were larger and capable of operating at much higher altitudes.

They all watched as the two Wasps set down about one-hundred meters away from them, thrusters so powerful, the air around the choppers began to ionize.

The doors slid open and a dozen QRF airmen and airwomen charged out of both choppers, rifles up, headed towards the dropship wreckage. A few of the combat medics that trailed behind them slowed to investigate the Wraith corpses that were littered everywhere.

Pinehurst turned to Matt with a cynical smirk. "Better late than never, I guess."

Matt shook his head in joyous disbelief.

The QRF's Crew Chief stepped into the dropship cabin, surveying the wreckage while trying to fathom how anyone could have survived. He was a brawny, thick-necked man who looked to be of Slovak descent. When he lifted his faceplate, a deep scar was visible. It trailed unevenly from his left eye down to the tip of his chin. "Who's Reeves?"

Matt stepped forward. "That would be me, sir."

"Apologies for the wait. We've been jammed up all week. Still have multiple fireteams out there who need assistance." His gaze drifted to the seven soldiers from Kilo Company now being assisted by his medics, also noting the scant weapons and ammo supplies Matt's team was packing. He then glanced at the Death Pony, which was still a giant ball of flame. "That Pony was already on the ground. How'd you bring it down?"

"I crash landed it."

The Crew Chief turned and looked at Matt with bewilderment. "You flew that thing?"

"For a while at least."

"The hell you doing flying a Death pony around?"

"Long story."

"Yeah, well, Hatchett's going to want to know all of it. Gather your squad, we take off in five."

"Roger that, sir."

As the Crew Chief turned and walked off to assist the other members of his team, Kapernock leaned in behind Matt. "I think after the shitty day we've had - especially you - we've earned a little downtime back at Rhino."

Overhearing Kapernock, one of the medics assisting Hernandez looked up while securing her gurney. "Don't bet on it. Command is gearing up to push into the Capital."

Kapernock snickered. "And they're more than welcome to. But I need my beauty asleep."

"You need a fuck-load more than sleep to look beautiful, Kapernock," quipped Hernandez. She was now rigged up to several intravenous fluid bags and a heart monitor. Another medic tinkered with a machine that was clamped around her wounded leg.

Kapernock replied his usual way and blew a kiss at her.

She hacked up a laugh.

"Gonna have to wait until the war's over until we catch up on any sleep," said the medic as he slung a large supply bag over his shoulder.

"You're assuming it's going to end," said Hernandez.

"Then we can sleep when we're dead."

Hernandez looked at Matt and the others. "Fuckin' hooah. Looks like we've got ourselves a potential Black Skull over here."

The medic gave a dismissive laugh as he continued to calibrate his medical equipment.

Matt approached Hernandez' gurney and grabbed her hand firmly. "Try not to bust his balls on the flight back, OK?"

"You know I can't promise that," she said with a devilish grin.

"See you back at base, soldier."

She nodded sleepily, her eyes glassy as a fresh dose of morphine began to course through her body. "You just make sure you get your ass on that Wasp, Matt."

He smiled and nodded. "Copy that, Sergeant. Never out of the fight."

"Never out of the fight," she replied, squeezing his hand tighter. A tear escaped down her left cheek, forging a clean trail through the blood and grime. Today was a day none of them would ever forget.

Matt watched the medics wheel her off towards one of the parked Wasps.

"Well done, Black Skulls," boomed an authoritative voice from behind them.

Matt, Pinehurst, Strack, and Kapernock all turned to see Hatchett standing there. They immediately snapped to attention.

Hatchett folded his arms behind his back and proceeded to move past them, calmly studying the cabin damage. "What remains of that Wraith unit is in full retreat. Our Destroyer is mopping up." He noticed the vacant troop seats, two of them stained with dark blood. He whipped around to face Matt, his flinty eyes boring into him. "Helluva day, son."

"Plenty more to go, sir."

"And you're good with that?"

"Yes, sir!"

Satisfied, Hatchett gave Matt a precise nod. "Excellent, because I have one last mission for you."

TWENTY

Operation Blue Trident
Outskirts of the Wraith Capital...

IT WAS NEARLY dusk when Matt lowered himself off the rooftop ledge as quietly as he could to shake out the tiny rock from his combat boot. It had been grinding into his right heel all day. He flicked it away then refastened his boot, looking out over the destroyed outskirts of the Capital from his recon position on top of a dilapidated building.

Even at dusk, Epsilon's sun stubbornly clung to the horizon, making the rubbled buildings out there shimmer like some insidious mirage.

"Can't see nothin.' Switchin' up my thermals," whispered Kapernock.

Matt blinked back to reality. Back to the mission. Back to hell.

Kapernock had been scanning the area with his rifle scope for nearly an hour, but nothing was registering. "Come on, come on, where are these assholes?" When he shifted position to scan another cluster of buildings, it caused some metallic debris to tumble off the edge of the roof.

It hit the promenade below with a loud clang that echoed across the street.

The four Black Skulls froze, breaths caught in each of their throats.

"Fer fuck's sake!" hissed Strack. "You got a death wish or something?"

Kapernock snorted, his eyes still scanning the partially destroyed buildings. "You keep running that pimply mouth of yours, Spot, I'm gonna put you to sleep and leave your ass out here. How's that for a death wish?"

"Guys, cut the shit-talk! Keep your heads in the game," ordered Matt. "Kapernock, don't stop cycling through your thermals until you find me something with a heartbeat."

"Roger that, sir."

It had been six days since Hatchett anointed Matt to lead this critical mission into what remained of the Wraith's Capital. So far, since their covert insertion, they had managed to remain undetected. Before Matt, and what remained of his squad were deployed, Hatchett's orbital cannons had rendered much of the city into nothing more than an endless sprawl of black debris. Yet, he suspected the small enemy compound they were targeting somehow remained unscathed and was still very much operational. Matt's primary mission was to locate and destroy it.

Easier said than done.

Matt was surprised how deserted the Capital appeared. At least on the surface. He knew there was probably no shortage of enemy infantry still hiding somewhere underground. The Wraith preferred to build down instead of up, with many of their dwellings cutting deep into the planet's mantle, so the overall damage inflicted upon their infantry units in this area would have most likely been minimal.

And while there were visible entranceways into most buildings, with the grander doors and archways being exclusive to government and military complexes, there were no windows on any structures that remained intact. None. For the entire time Matt had been here, he was yet to see a building or structure with a single window or viewport of some kind.

"I got 'em, I got 'em! Wraith at my twelve. They're cloaked. Must be two dozen," Kapernock whispered excitedly.

"What's your spectrum setting?" asked Pinehurst.

"Two-zero-eight," Kapernock replied. "Doesn't show up on our usual range threshold. Sneaky fuckers."

Matt slithered across to Kapernock on his belly to get a better vantage point. He raised the scope on his assault rifle to his faceplate, scanning the gaping valley of rubble.

Everything was eerily quiet as his reticles hovered over the roof of an adjacent structure. He then switched to Kapernock's spectrum setting, and sure enough, activity sprung to life.

There was a massive mobile artillery cannon fixed to the roof. Its scorched barrel towered into the sky like some blackened femur bone. A rabble of Wraith soldiers teemed around its circular base, preparing to unleash hell.

Matt instinctively ducked his head as the cannon began firing bursts of charged ions. The clap of each shot made his ribs shudder, the thick cushioning inside his helmet doing little to stop his ears from ringing. This type of Wraith weapon was effectively a long-range battery armament, capable of wiping out a base like Camp Rhino with a single shot. Whatever they had begun firing on, Matt was certain it was a vital USC asset of some kind. They needed to shut this thing down yesterday.

He spun around to Strack. "Not hoping for a miracle but call it in anyway. See if we can get some fire on that crew."

"Roger," replied Strack. He began triangulating their position on the sleek communications device strapped to his left forearm. "Archangel, this is Saber-One. We are looking at an enemy artillery compound. Yankee Zulu Sector, two-two-six-seven-three. Blue Force

Tracker uploading. Target is qualified. Spectrum heading two-zero-eight. Requesting orbital munitions support, over."

Bars of static pulsed across their faceplates as they sat there, waiting for a reply from their audio feeds.

"*Ah, that's a negative, Saber-one. Orbital munitions support is a no-go at this time. I repeat, orbital munitions support is a no-go at this time,*" said the officer on comms.

Matt breathed an exhausted sigh and dropped his head. *Shit.*

The others groaned.

Strack immediately closed the channel. Emitting any type of high-frequency signal for too long out in the field wasn't a good idea, especially this deep inside enemy territory.

"Fuck it, maybe we should find some better cover and dig in for a while longer. At least until orbital support does become available," Kapernock said.

Pinehurst looked at him and scoffed. "Kapernock, what part of *we're on our own* don't you understand?"

"You're right," Matt grumbled, doing his best to keep his own frustration in check. "Any support we had was used up three days before we got here."

Kapernock shook his head. "Something doesn't feel right on this one."

Pinehurst gave him a terse look. "Dude, we're stuck on some rock, thousands of light-years from Earth, fighting a war we're not winning. No shit something doesn't feel right."

"You know what I mean. I just think— I don't know, maybe we could wait until they can get an armored drone out to our position. That's gotta be better than nothing, right?"

"War will be over by then," replied Matt.

"Hey, it's your call. But if we get spotted by one of their snipers again—"

"Then we take it out," Matt interrupted sharply. "We do our job, just like we've been doing since the first day we arrived here." He signaled for Kapernock to turn around before he could respond, unzipping his supply bag to pull out a thermal grenade.

Shaped like a gridiron, they were small in comparison to other explosive devices used in the field, but they emitted a significant blast radius. One grenade would be powerful enough to take out that entire artillery unit.

There was tense silence among them as Matt readied himself for the attack. He secured the grenade inside one of his supply pouches then gingerly craned his neck over the edge of the damaged rooftop.

With a little luck, he would be able to skitter down to the promenade below and make his way along the street without being spotted.

"Pinehurst, you're with me. Let's move out."

Pinehurst gave Matt an earnest nod, but the look in his eyes told a different story. Clearly, he wasn't too thrilled. Nevertheless, he had his orders. He began to carefully make his way down the mountain of rubble on his side, careful not to slip on loose debris.

Matt turned to Kapernock and Strack, his blue eyes, bristling underneath his faceplate's HUD read-outs. "Hold fire until we engage. And remember - aim for the smaller plates on their armor. Seems to be a weak spot. Once that cannon is down, we haul ass to our exfill. Hooah?"

"Hooah," the two of them replied in a unified whisper-shout."

Matt then turned and dangled his legs over the edge of the slanted rooftop, ready to follow Pinehurst down. But before he dismounted, he took off his left armored-glove and quickly fished out a silver necklace, kissing the gold wedding band that was attached to it. He then tucked it back underneath his chest armor and slipped his glove back on.

As he began to inch down the rubble slope, a feeling of dread began to calcify in his stomach. What they were about to do was most likely suicide.

Matt knew it, and so did his men.

TWENTY-ONE

MATT AND PINEHURST moved swiftly along the street, weaving between large mounds of rubble that dripped molten slag.

The skyscraper-sized columns of choking ash that drifted up from the ground was a testament to the power the USC's orbital munitions were capable of projecting. From what Matt could see, much of the Capital was still burning, days after it had been struck.

"Eyes open. Watch our six," Matt said in a tense whisper.

"On it." Pinehurst pivoted to cover their rear.

They were approaching a fork in the street which branched off into several triangular promenades. Matt was already familiar with this area. He had studied orbital reconnaissance images of the Capital after his mission briefing. The Wraith had a strange architectural penchant for designing their buildings in triangular shapes. The entire Capital was basically a cluster of smaller triangles nestled inside a much larger one. Prior to the war, the Capital would have roughly been the size of Manhattan. A Manhattan where every building was entirely featureless and black. A Manhattan without a single window or viewport.

When they arrived at the fork, Matt gingerly edged along a crumbling wall until he reached the corner of it.

Pinehurst followed, still keeping his sights trained on their rear.

Matt peered around, the scope of his assault rifle level with his right eye.

The compound loomed in the distance. Wraith heat signatures flared into brilliant hues of green and blue as they continued to fire their artillery cannon. The thunderclap of each shot was almost deafening this close.

Matt slowly edged back, turning to Pinehurst. "We're never going to get near them without a distraction. Deploy your Sentry."

Pinehurst slung his rifle over his shoulder and clipped off a brick-like device from his belt. He placed it on the ground before them, then tapped some commands into the small holographic display hovering above his forearm plate.

The brick opened, transforming into a small Sentry Turret, mounted on four metallic pincers.

"Move it up," whispered Matt, eyes locking onto the compound again.

Pinehurst quickly entered some coordinates and the turret began to hobble away from their position in a sideways crab-walk, heading towards the open rotunda at the end of the street.

Matt watched it come to a halt, now facing the compound as its target identification systems whirred to life.

These automated turrets were only tiny, but they packed a lot of grunt - capable of firing a thousand ionized rounds per minute, with a muzzle velocity that spanned over two thousand feet. It was enough firepower to distract the Wraith while Matt and Pinehurst flanked their position.

"Once it starts firing, we're gonna have about five seconds to reach the other side of that street."

Pinehurst nodded, swallowing his dry throat.

Matt could see the fear coiled in his friend's eyes. He was terrified. Matt was too. He put a firm hand on his armored shoulder plate.

"Hey, we've got this OK? Just keep that scope glued to your eye, and don't let them flank us. You good, brother?"

Pinehurst sucked in a deep breath and nodded again. "Yeah. Fuck it, let's do it."

By the time either of them could process what happened next, they had already been blown off their feet.

A concealed Wraith unit who had been providing overwatch for the artillery crew began firing on their position having detected the turret. A barrage of molten-blue pulse rounds strafed the street, chewing up rock and debris with a deafening rip. The turret was obliterated in a flash, its internal ammo-core detonating with the force of a small bomb.

Matt was blown back by the explosion, slamming hard into a pile of rubble. The force of the blast had ripped the assault rifle from his grip, but miraculously, the thermal grenade was still secure inside his supply pouch.

He rolled over to see Pinehurst laying on the opposite side of the street, minus both his legs.

"Pinehurst! Just hold on!" he yelled. He got back onto his feet when another concussive burst of enemy fire crackled into the ground, causing him to scramble for cover behind a small wall. "Motherfuckers...!"

Coated in dust and debris, Pinehurst groaned as he sluggishly lifted his faceplate and raised his head, looking down in shock at the two mangled stumps that were once his legs. He was bleeding out so fast, the blast craters surrounding him were now scarlet-red potholes. He screamed for Matt to help him. "Matt— oh, Jesus— fuuuuck! Maaaatt!"

But Matt had other problems. The Wraith unit was now headed their way.

He peered up over his cover to see them materializing through the smoky haze. There were four of them. All armed with fist-guns and Reaper-rifles.

They descended upon Pinehurst, looking down at him as nothing more than a temporary inconvenience. There was no way Matt could help him. All he could do was watch in horror as one of the Wraith's fired a round into Pinehurst's face, incinerating him into a swirling cloud of ash.

Matt paled, feeling his legs buckling underneath him. He wanted to unleash an anguished scream, but somehow his instincts took control and he managed to staunch it. Assuming he could survive the next few minutes, there would be plenty of time to grieve. But now was not that time.

At that moment, he remembered Kapernock and Strack were still on the rooftop. From their position, they could clearly see everything unfolding on the street below, so why weren't they providing any supporting fire?

He spun around to face the rooftop and his question was immediately answered.

It was now a smoldering crater. Their position had also been compromised. The churning plumes of thick black smoke implied neither of them would have survived such a devastating strike.

Matt spun back to the approaching enemy, his jaw firmly set. He was close enough to hear one of them barking orders to the other soldiers. He didn't need to understand their dialect to know he had about five seconds of play left before they would spot him.

He pulled out the thermal grenade from his pouch and armed it. "If I don't get to go home, you bastards ain't going to either…" Then, he popped up from behind the wall and tossed the charge directly in front of the Wraith unit.

It detonated before they even knew it was there, the explosion vaporized them in an instant.

The blast-wave smashed into the wall Matt was crouching behind, lifting him off his feet once again. He was sprayed with sharp stone, fragments of the wall peppering his armored breastplate with the force of a hundred tiny bullets. He cracked hard against the base of an overhead beam.

The last thing Matt remembered was looking up to see the top-half of the beam plummeting straight down onto him.

TWENTY-TWO

THE BEDROOM CLOSET was stuffy and cramped. Karen Reeves dozed lightly, wedged between a muddle of clothes and stacked boxes.

Her one-year-old toddler, Ally, was also with her, strapped into a car seat that was perched atop a pile of clothes.

They had been hiding in here for the past five hours. Karen had turned the closet into a DIY bomb-shelter, making sure there was enough blankets, snack food, and water to last a few days.

After Matt had left for work, she flicked on the TV to see the breaking news. Surfing through every channel, it was nothing but grim-faced Anchors relaying the same information. Some of them barely spoke above a whisper, their voices jittery and weak as they struggled to comprehend the information they were relaying to the camera; a foreign military force had brazenly attacked the United States. Within minutes, it seemed these invaders were everywhere across the nation, taking authorities completely by surprise. One of the local Anchors, visibly shaken, rose from her news desk and walked off during a live broadcast after learning that Washington D.C. had gone completely dark.

It was also evident these invaders were not of terrestrial origin.

Karen watched with equal disbelief and horror as amateur phone footage from the Griffith Observatory showed a massive Wraith fleet decimating downtown Los Angeles. There were at least eight ships floating silently over the city, each one three times the size of an aircraft carrier.

She had tried calling Matt and his parents numerous times throughout the morning, as well as her own parents in Pittsburgh. But every fiber line and wireless network across the county was grossly overloaded, making it impossible to connect. Once the electricity went out, she thought about loading up the car and taking off with Ally to search for Matt. But based on what the local news had shown earlier, venturing outside was far too dangerous.

Karen had no choice but to stay inside the house and wait for Matt to return. Assuming he was still alive.

TWENTY-THREE

MATT JOLTED awake from his dream, his forehead beaded with cold sweat. While he waited to gather his bearings, he breathed in the cool stale air through his nose. There was a metallic tang to it. Something about it seemed familiar. As his bleary eyes began to focus more, he remembered where he was.

He was crammed into the back of a USC troop shuttle, strapped into a jump-seat, heading home to Earth. Harrisonville, Kentucky, to be exact.

There was a long row of troops facing him, with several rows behind. The thick harnesses around his shoulders and chest felt suffocating. He couldn't help but think how good it was going to feel to finally be free of this steel bucket, and to feel the warm kiss of Earth's sun on his skin. He also longed to breathe fresh air again. Real air. Not Epsilon's murky oxygen, or the recycled O2 he'd been sucking on for the past year.

Matt had embarked home to Earth from *Salvation,* a decommissioned medical frigate that permanently orbited the Moon. The ship served as both a deployment and arrival station for all USC personnel. It was the last port of call for troops returning home from interstellar travel, and the first port of call for troops deploying to Epsilon. These fresh troop batches would spend a week on Salvation as they prepped for their year-long deep-freeze.

A small recovery team had carefully awoken Matt from his own cryo-sleep two weeks earlier, yet he still felt exhausted and brittle. He caught a couple of troops sitting on the opposite side of the cabin grinning at him. They knew exactly what he was experiencing. Amnesia and fever dreams were common side-effects. The symptoms would fade over time, but it usually took a few weeks for the brain to completely settle down as the body continued recuperating.

The purpose of freezing troops on the return journey home wasn't just for dealing with long distances of space travel - it also acted as a healing procedure. Long-term exposure to Epsilon's harsh environment was damaging to human cells, so before troops were put into their cryo-pods, they had to bathe in a substance commonly referred to as *Curd*.

Rich in a variety of minerals and vitamins, Curd prepared human tissue for the deep freeze. It also helped heal wounds on the journey home by accelerating tissue regeneration. But Matt found the entire process of Curd baths absolutely disgusting. He was not alone. *Imagine spending an entire day marinating in a giant tub of lukewarm snot that also happens to smell like an outdoor fish market*, a rather grumpy Deployment Officer once said to Matt on Salvation when asked to describe them in more detail.

The post-cryo medication they had been giving him to help with blood circulation also wasn't helping much. Aside from making him bilious, it also gave him crippling stomach pains. He straightened in his seat, thinking he may pitch forward and puke on his lap. But he managed to staunch it, the quiver in his jaw subsiding as he took some deep, steady breaths.

"You OK there, sir?" said the young soldier seated next to him.

Matt rubbed his eyes and nodded. "Yeah, I'm fine. Think I'm still thawing out."

The young soldier grinned, adjusting the harness that crossed his chest. "I know what you mean, sir. A year is a long time to be a Popsicle."

"Doubt I'll ever look at an ice tray the same way again," Matt replied. They both shared a chuckle before the harsh shrill of an alarm echoed throughout the cabin.

"All flight protocols are go. Prepare for re-entry," announced the shuttle pilot over the crackly intercom.

The shuttle began to tilt. Matt craned his head around to the nearest viewport. The other troops did the same.

The curvature of the Earth came into view, filling their eyes with a radiant blue they had not seen in six years. A couple of troops whistled and cheered. Some started clapping.

Matt smiled, but it faded as a grim thought suddenly crossed his mind; every transport shuttle housed a storage area below deck, specifically for the caskets returning home. Those families on Earth who got to bury their loved ones were considered lucky. Sadly, most families only ever received crisply folded flags. Due to the devastating weaponry used in this conflict, it was not uncommon for entire battlefields to be rendered as nothing more than wastelands of ash, making it impossible to locate the remains of Earth's fallen soldiers.

The families of Matt's squad would also not be receiving any caskets. He had spent countless hours trying to rationalize the loss of the twenty-two Praetorians he once commanded. Being the sole survivor of the Black Skulls didn't feel fair, or just, but it was the way the chips had fallen. Matt often wondered if he would ever be able to accept it. The guilt that had anchored inside him did not seem to be in a hurry to go anywhere.

The troop's cheers and whistles intensified when the iridescent glow of Earth was blotted out by the *Sentinel* - a huge unmanned Intelligence and Reconnaissance platform which was designed to stay in orbit indefinitely. Its sole purpose was to track the many USC assets scattered around the solar system, as well as monitor for any potential enemy craft.

Matt caught the striking insignia branded across its hull flash past the viewport; an Eagle clutching a wreath, with the Latin words, *Adiutorio Tuo Vincemus* underneath it. 'We Will Prevail.'

Suddenly, Matt was pushed back hard into his seat by the intense G-forces as the pilot engaged the shuttle's thrusters. The fiery orange glow from outside now filled every viewport. Metal moaned and shuddered.

Matt closed his eyes, doing his best to block out the rattling girder above him. He tried focusing on his daughter. A mix of anxiousness and excitement started to replace the sickly feeling in his stomach. He missed Ally beyond words. She was everything to him. But what would she look like after all these years? She was only four when he left her. Would she even recognize him? Would he recognize her?

Everything in the shuttle began to vibrate harder now. As Matt sat there, hoping it wouldn't suddenly break apart during re-entry, Karen crossed his mind. She did every day, but today was different. Today was special. He began the usual ritual of fidgeting with his wedding ring whenever he thought of her. Since leaving the war, he had also returned the ring to its rightful place on his finger. Karen would have expected that.

Eyes still closed, Matt tilted his head back in his seat and breathed out a sigh. After six grueling years, it was hard to believe he was nearly home. It was even harder to believe he was still alive.

TWENTY-FOUR

MATT STOOD in line with the other troops as the shuttle's bay doors split open with a hydraulic whine. Autumn sunlight flooded the cabin, and cheers could be heard from the waiting crowd outside. He slung his duffel bag over his shoulder and marched single-file down the bay door ramp.

As Matt walked out onto the vast stretch of tarmac, he saw three other shuttles taxiing towards the spaceport, with another three about to land.

The crowd standing behind the barriers was huge. Hundreds of families, friends, and loved ones waved and whistled at the first batch of troops. Some held up giant homemade banners welcoming their sons and daughters back to Earth. Nearby, a small band belted out a stilted rendition of the official USC Anthem.

"...From every corner of the globe. We stand as one. The enemy feels our might. Our brothers and sisters stay in the fight. For we are victorious. On land and shore. In air and void. On every fighting field. You will find the USC shield..."

Matt scanned the cheering crowd, searching for a recognizable face. A few civilians slapped him on the back as he passed through them, thanking him for his service. There were also some boos in the crowd. A small group of anti-war protesters had been relegated by port security to the far end of the tarmac. They held up placards and holographic signs opposing the USC while they chanted anti-war slogans.

During his tour, Matt had heard about the growing list of activist bodies back on Earth who were vehemently opposed to sending children off into space to die. They also argued that the growing concern of a second invasion being ginned up by the media was nothing more than warmongering propaganda that did nothing for the planet's population, let alone the millions of soldiers who had already been slaughtered since the USC launched its counter-strike. Of course, the USC combated these groups by spending billions each year lobbying various governments around the world, reiterating the notion that defunding this interstellar war would result in nothing less than the total annihilation of the human species.

"Dad?"

The voice behind him was faint. Matt spun around to see Ally running through the thick crowd towards him. It took him a few seconds to process the fact that he was actually looking at his daughter. "Ally?" he yelled, his eyes filling with tears. He dropped his duffel bag as she leaped into his arms. He scooped her up off her feet, hugging her tightly. "Oh, I missed you so much, Al."

"Me too," she said softly.

Tears streaked down Matt's cheeks as he nuzzled against her neck. He didn't want to let go of her ever again.

"Are you home for good now?" she asked, hoping the answer was a firm *yes*.

"I'm home, sweetheart. I'm home."

Matt pulled away to get a better look at her. The strawberry-blond locks had become fuller and redder since he last saw her. She looked even more like her mother now. She was almost a teenager. "Wow... I can't believe how much you've grown."

Ally smiled coyly, her arms still wrapped around Matt's neck.

"Yeah, that's what Grandma says. Says I'm already too big for my boots."

Matt laughed and planted a huge kiss on her cheek.

"Matt!"

Matt and Ally turned to see his parents, Lynette and Jacob Reeves, pushing through the crowd towards them.

They were wholesome country folk, both in their mid-fifties. High school sweethearts, despite such a thing being a rarity by the time they graduated. After marrying, they were both content with life in the country - working on the family farm and raising a child. For them, that was the last bastion of a simpler time. They often joked how they had been born into the completely wrong era.

"Oh, my son. I'm so glad you're home," Jacob said, his eyes welled with tears.

The four of them embraced in a group hug.

TWENTY-FIVE

JACOB'S old 2040 model Chevy Tahoe cruised along the State highway, more modern and sleeker vehicles zipping past them in the opposite left-hand lane.

The right-hand lane was exclusively for the big, unmanned livestock rigs and hydrogen-fueled semi-trailers that glided on rails of light. These lanes were also reserved for the automated delivery drones which constantly teemed above, moving between different towns and cities.

Aside from the groundbreaking military advancements of the past decade or so, the invasion, and subsequent conflict that followed, had stifled much of man's technological advancements. However, post-invasion, there were visible signs of increasing progress across the world, especially in the transportation industries. Despite that, Jacob was one of the few people left who preferred driving their vehicle the old way, manually. Even though the new automated hands-free electric models had flawless safety records, he wasn't too fond of putting his life in the hands of some foreign-coded Artificial Intelligence. Jacob liked the idea that a man could still plot his own course in life, even if it was something as minuscule as driving an outdated vehicle that ran on ethanol.

Matt was sitting in the back seat with Ally, watching the automated grain harvesters that hovered over the vast biofuel corn fields running parallel to the highway. They were behemoths. Reminiscent of the huge bucket and excavator machines that were once used for mining, but easily three times the size.

His gaze drifted upwards, squinting at the blue sky overhead. The day could not have been any more beautiful. The air was mild and crisp, and the sky was dotted with fluffy white clouds. He gently rested his head against the window and closed his eyes, savoring the warmth of the sun on his face. After enduring Epsilon's oppressive humidity for the past four years, it was quite easy to appreciate the little things, like a mild Autumn day in Kentucky.

Ally's giggle caused Matt to glance down at her. She was excitedly messaging her friend on her phone's holographic interface about her Dad's arrival home. He couldn't help but smile.

After another hour of driving, Jacob turned off the state highway and headed into Shelby County, eventually turning up the narrow dirt road that snaked all the way to their old farmhouse.

It sat perched atop a hill, surrounded by bur-oak trees. There was an empty field to the left, which was once a dryland pasture filled with livestock. For the most part, the property was barren and dusty, but the farmhouse still held onto its original idyllic charm.

Upon seeing it come into view, Matt thought it hadn't changed at all in six years. It was exactly how he remembered it. He was home.

Jacob's Tahoe pulled up outside the house. Matt opened his passenger-side door and was greeted by the family Bloodhound.

"Clyde! Aw, I missed you too, buddy."

Ally giggled with delight when Clyde barked with excitement and leaped onto Matt, slobbering all over him with licks and sniffs. Matt was nearly knocked clean off his feet.

Jacob watched on as Clyde twisted its lanky body around Matt's legs while sniffing him, tail still wagging furiously. "You know, he was already sitting at the front door before we left this morning. He never does that. I think he knew you were coming home."

Matt, Ally, and Jacob sat at the kitchen table, munching on traditional hot brown sandwiches that Lynette had prepared earlier. They were Matt's favorite, having first eaten one at the Kentucky State Fair when he was a kid.

Lynette grinned with amusement, watching Matt gleefully chow it all down. Every now and then, the soldiers in Matt's regiment would talk about the wonderful home-cooked meals their parents or loved ones made them back on Earth. Matt always made a point to mention Lynette's hot brown sandwiches. After surviving on standard-issue rations for so long, he'd forgotten how amazing these sandwiches tasted.

Ally climbed down from her chair and disappeared for a moment, reappearing with a pile of sketches she had printed out on smart paper from her tablet. She held them up to Matt.

"Oh, cool." Matt carefully spread them out across the table while chewing his food. They were basic digital brush illustrations of various farm animals, slightly animated, but they clearly showed Ally possessed a natural talent. "These are good, Al. I mean, you've really gotten good."

"Not bad, huh? In the last year, she's really started to flourish," Jacob said, before sipping his glass of cherry soda.

Ally pulled out another piece of paper she was hiding behind her back, and gingerly handed it to Matt. "I did this one for you."

This rendering wasn't created digitally. It was a pencil sketch of Matt in his USC uniform, brandishing his assault rifle. Matt could tell she had spent a lot of time refining the sketch. The level of detail she had managed to capture from memory was beyond impressive, especially for a ten-year-old. He studied it for another moment, amazed.

"Do you like it?" asked Ally, unsure if he did.

Matt looked at her with a proud smile. "Are you kidding? I love it. In fact, I'm going to have it framed. How about we drive into town tomorrow morning. You can help me pick one out."

Ally nodded excitedly. She loved that idea. As Matt went back to gobbling down the last of his sandwich, she gave a relieved look to Lynette.

Lynette smiled and winked back at her.

TWENTY-SIX

MATT WANDERED into the living room with Clyde, while Jacob and Ally helped Lynette clear the kitchen table.

He approached a mahogany wall cabinet that was the centerpiece of the room, his eyes drifting over the framed family photos that adorned its shelves. Each one chronicled an important event; Matt's own baby photos, Ally's birth, family vacations, Christmas, Easter, Thanksgiving, Matt in his police uniform. There were also photos of Matt heading off to basic, dressed in USC fatigues.

Then, his gaze landed on one particular photo which caused his breath to catch in his throat.

It was of himself and Karen, taken in Hawaii during their honeymoon, years before the invasion. They were in the surf together, cheek-to-cheek, young and madly in love. Excited about what the future held for them.

Matt picked it up, his eyes vacant. Everything captured in that photo seemed so distant to him now. So lost. So alien. He hardly recognized himself.

He turned to see Jacob standing behind him, twirling his car keys.

Jacob drove towards town with Matt sitting next to him. Matt pressed a small button on his passenger-side door and his window slid down. He stuck his head out, allowing the country air to fill his lungs.

Jacob glanced over and smiled. "Good, huh?"

Matt closed his eyes and breathed deeply. "You have no idea."

The engine in Jacob's Tahoe suddenly coughed and splattered. Jacob pumped the gas pedal. "Ah... she's getting a bit temperamental in her old age." He caught Matt looking at him with a smirk. "Don't even say it."

"I can't help it. I just— seriously, dad. This thing is ancient. It's older than you."

Jacob grinned, his eyes back on the road. "So, you're happy to walk all the way home then?"

"I'm just saying, maybe it's time you bought a new car."

Jacob snickered. "For your information, young man, this car is somewhat the family heirloom."

Matt groaned and rolled his eyes. "Oh, God, here we go."

"It was my Grandpa's SUV for many years. Back when us Reeves used to grow soybeans. Real soybeans too, not that genetically modified crap."

"Dad, it costs a fortune to maintain, and they don't even make cars like this anymore. They haven't for years."

There was a beat of silence as Jacob chewed on that before he responded. "Yeah, you're probably right. I'm just being overly nostalgic. But sometimes it's hard to let go of certain things, you know? And this car — it reminds me of a time when this country made things. Made things that actually mattered. Big things."

Matt turned to face his window again, thick snarls of his brown hair flapping wildly in the wind as he watched cars zip by in the opposite lane. "They still do, dad. I'm sure you've seen the ship I came home on."

Jacob's expression darkened. "I'm talking about a long time ago. Before the invasion. Before the war. Things are different now."

Matt's eyes narrowed as he looked out over the never-ending sprawl of corn and wheat fields to see a dark, ominous shape looming on the horizon.

It was an enormous Wraith battleship. USC forces had brought it down right over a cornfield. Its skeletal hull sat lopsided, partially embedded into the earth. Its mile-high antenna towered into the sky like the barb of some giant stingray.

Matt kept his eyes on it as it passed by. Jacob was indeed right. Things were different now.

TWENTY-SEVEN

MATT AND JACOB sat huddled in a corner booth at the local bar, nursing their second beer each.

"...And the grave?" said Matt, looking down at his glass solemnly.

Jacob breathed deep and gave a reassuring nod. "It's fine. Lynette makes sure there's fresh flowers every week. I try and visit as often as I can... I thought maybe you would've—"

"I will," said Matt, sipping his glass. "I'll visit. I just— you know— I wanted to take a day or two to readjust."

"I understand. I imagine that's probably going to take some time, Matt."

"Matt's eyes flicked up to his father. "Yeah. Everything will."

Jacob ran a hand idly through his salt-and-pepper beard, his eyes staying on Matt. "I can only imagine what you saw on that godforsaken rock."

Matt's jaw clenched, there was a pause of silence between them.

Jacob noticed his son's eyes were starting to well with tears. He reached over the table and put a comforting hand on his arm. "Hey, I didn't mean to—"

"It's OK," said Matt, smearing away the tears from his eyes. He composed himself before continuing. "I had some... there was quite a few men and women who died under my command."

Jacob shook his head and groaned. "Ah, shit. I'm sorry, Matt. I really am."

Matt took another sip of his beer, savoring its bitterness. He put the glass down, silently galvanizing himself to continue. "We lost a lot of good people, dad. Just so many... all gone." He trailed off, eyes hardening as darker memories started to creep into his mind. "It's those damn Wraiths... they're like drones - programmed to keep on fighting us until we've been wiped from existence. They'll never stop, dad. I know that for a fact. Assuming we even last, we'll be in this war for centuries to come."

"Ten years later, and we're still cleaning up the mess those bastards left behind," Jacob snarled. "I just don't understand these USC lackeys and politicians." He leaned in closer, his elbows planted firmly on the table.

Matt looked at the large vein protruding from his forehead which had flared into a squiggly line. Whenever he saw that particular vein appear, he knew his father was really ticked off about something. Fortunately, it was a rare occurrence.

"You know what the best prevention for this war is? We start ignoring those spineless regulation committees and nuke their planet. Turn it into a giant fucking ball of glass!" Jacob leaned back from the table, realizing how worked up he'd gotten himself.

"Dad, their planet was already dying before we showed up. That's probably why they came here in the first place. All a bunch of nukes would do is make them more determined to conquer Earth again. That's assuming we could even fire any off before they deflected them back onto us. It's their technology. Sure, we can mimic a lot of its capabilities now, but for the most part, it's still way more advanced than anything we've managed to reverse engineer. We just don't know enough about it yet."

For a long moment, Jacob's gaze lingered on his beer, his eyes softening to become a vacant stare. "I tell you, when we got word they pulled you out of that rubble still alive, Lynette and I must've cried non-stop for an entire week..." He looked up and caught Matt watching him. "I'm sorry, son— I get a few beers into me—"

"It's fine, you're just venting. Trust me, I'm glad they did find me."

Jacob nodded, his lip quivering. He looked away, trying not to make too much of a scene in front of his kid. "You ever need to get something off your chest, Matt... you come to me, you hear? I'm your father. Anything at all, you can talk to me about it."

Matt nodded. "Well, there are some things I obviously can't talk about— certain things I saw, certain things I did. But if the day ever comes when I can talk about them, I promise I will."

Jacob continued to fight back his tears. "I'll always be proud of what you did there, Matt. Your mother too. You're a good kid. Good kid."

Matt smiled at him with a nod. "Thanks, dad."

There was another beat between them while Jacob restored his composure.

"Hey, what do you say we grab some pizza for the ride home?" Matt said, excitedly. "Oh, man, you know how long it's been since I've had a decent slice?"

Jacob was still a little teary, but he returned a warm smile. "Sounds good."

They finished their drinks, but before Matt slid out of the booth, he took a moment to admire a tiny inscription that was key-carved into the booth's wooden paneling. It was faded, but he could still make it out:

Matt loves Karen 4ever.

He remembered the night he did it. Karen and he were both a little drunk having just come from a mutual friend's birthday party. It was also the night Matt knew he wanted to ask her to marry him. He wasn't a cop at that time, and for years after the original owner had passed on, he felt bad about vandalizing everyone's favorite bar in town.

As he gently ran his fingers over the grooves of the inscription he smiled to himself, remembering how happy Karen was back then. How hopeful she was about the future. How during that night, over the rowdy live music, she had leaned over to him and whispered into his ear that she loved him. The very next day, they broke the engagement news to their parents.

"Earth to Matt" yelled Jacob, standing by the front entrance of the bar. "You coming or what?"

Matt blinked back to the present. "Yeah, wait up." He slid out of the booth and followed Jacob to his Tahoe.

TWENTY-EIGHT

MATT KNEW something was wrong before he and Jacob even reached the house.

As they pulled up, Clyde was at the porch door, barking furiously at something outside. Lynette had him by the collar and was struggling to hold him back.

Matt hopped out of Jacob's car holding two large pizza boxes. "What's up with him?"

"I don't know," said Lynette. "He started going crazy about a minute before you arrived."

Matt turned and looked out across the field to see a bright light rapidly approaching in the sky. Over Clyde's barking, he could hear the faint, yet unmistakable thump of hypersonic rotors. He turned to Jacob and handed him the pizzas. "Go inside with Mom and Ally."

Jacob took them, but his eyes were fixed on the approaching light. "What is that?"

"Dad, just do it."

Jacob turned to him a bewildered look. "Matt, I'm not gonna—"

"Dad. Go!" Matt gently ushered Jacob towards the house. "I'll be fine."

Clyde was still barking rabidly as Ally appeared behind Lynette. "Daddy?"

"It's OK, Al. Stay inside with Grandma and Grandpa."

Matt hopped the low wire fence and began walking out across the field to meet the incoming Helo. He could tell by the sound of its rotors it was a *V-428 Valor*. Matt had seen them operating on Epsilon numerous times, but on Earth, they were usually reserved for transporting USC brass.

It flew low, skimming across the field before touching down a hundred yards from Matt.

Two armed Praetorians hopped out, followed by General Tanner Adderson. The array of service medals that gleamed across the breast of his uniform were visually striking in the fading light of dusk. Matt recognized him immediately. Adderson's lantern-jawed features and granite eyes were known to every troop who had served since the invasion. He was a living legend. His victory at *Maelstrom Point*, where he single-handedly drove back the Wraith and captured a major compound, had inspired an entire generation of Americans to enlist and serve. There were vague rumors he had retired from active duty, along with unconfirmed reports he had been assigned to head up some type of top-secret weapons program. Whatever the case, Matt figured he wasn't just dropping by to say hello. Furthermore, Matt had already been officially debriefed after arriving on Salvation, so this was highly irregular.

Matt stiffened his posture and saluted.

Adderson saluted back. "Sergeant First Class Reeves, I'm General Tanner Adderson." His gravelly voice crackled over the rotor-wash.

"Yes, sir. I know who you are," Matt replied, struggling to hide the awe in his eyes. "It's an honor."

"Thank you."

How can I help you, sir?" Matt noticed the pilot had not shut off the engine yet, and the two Praetorians were also fanned out across the field in sentry positions, adding to the urgency on display.

Adderson cut straight to the chase. "I need you to come with us, son. The future of this planet depends on it."

TWENTY-NINE

MATT SAT in a small briefing room, studying an eerie surveillance image on the holoscreen that gently floated above his table.

Adderson stood behind him, his hawkish eyes bristling with grave concern. They were in a secure building at the northernmost end of Fort Pennington, in Richmond, Kentucky.

The Wraith ship on-screen was hard to make out. Not from the image resolution, but because it was partially hidden by a thick cluster of icy rocks. The section that was visible, looked like a pine cone coated in white ash. The image began zooming out - enough to reveal that the ship was hiding in a tiny section of Saturn's ring system. It was an area, perhaps no bigger than a mile in diameter.

"We don't know how long they've been watching us. Or how they managed to get this close without detection."

"You think the Wraith are preparing for another invasion, sir?"

Adderson took a seat opposite Matt at the table. "Oh, I don't think they ever stopped their invasion. It was merely on pause." He worked his jaw before continuing. "I was recently reminded of a famous speech President Ronald Reagan once gave The United Nations. Have you ever watched it?"

"No, sir," Matt replied.

"It's fascinating. Reagan talked about mankind being forced to unite when confronted with the threat of an alien invasion..." Anderson snickered. "Little did he know, sixty-one years later the words he spoke that day would come true. The moment the Wraith arrived, we forgot all our worldly squabbles. Humans had no choice but to learn to trust each other. Perhaps for the first time ever. In some strange way, despite the hundreds of millions of lives that were lost during that attack, we gained something back the Wraith couldn't account for. A sense of community. A sense of purpose. Not only did we begin to think about our place in the universe as a species, we began to act on it..." Adderson caught Matt watching him curiously, and could tell he was starting to wonder where this was all headed. "We're losing millions of lives each year on Epsilon... I'm not sure how many millions more we can keep sending before there's no one left to fight." Adderson paused, his eyes still firmly locked on Matt. "I don't think we can't face another attack like the first one. They nearly wiped us out. It's going to be decades before this planet fully recovers."

"But what about all our new military advancements?" asked Matt.

Adderson shrugged. "I'm not discounting them. China has made some significant breakthroughs recently. So has India and Japan. But testing them at a proving ground is one thing. Having them fully operational off-world is an entirely different matter. That takes time, Matt. A lot of time." Adderson motioned to the screen in front of them. "And as you can see, time is something we don't have anymore."

Matt nodded in agreement. "So, you want me to take out that surveillance ship?"

"Actually, no. I don't."

Matt frowned with confusion, shifting in his seat.

Adderson gave another subtle wave of his hand.

The photo of a man appeared on screen. He looked to be in his mid-sixties. The spectacles he wore, coupled with the thin, wispy comb-over and greying beard, gave him a rather bookish, nerdy demeanor.

Adderson continued. "Weeks after the Wraith retreated, an Aid Relief team working at a refugee camp in Nevada discovered a journal buried under a pile of rubble. The owner of that journal was Dr. Michael Rossiter - the man you're looking at here. He was a Military Virologist overseeing a highly classified defense program. That was until he was killed during the final days of the invasion."

"Bio-weapons," added Matt.

Adderson nodded sternly. "Once the Wraith showed up, the USC began looking at ways to weaponize various pathogens. Of course, the problem was always going to be - how could we use them against our enemy without wiping ourselves out?"

Adderson waved at the screen again and a photo of a hard drive appeared, wrapped in something similar to a crime scene evidence bag. The plastic casing had considerable damage, its edges charred black.

"The world lost a lot of brilliant minds when the Wraith attacked us. But what's particularly interesting about Rossiter is what he left behind. There were only a few terabytes of data recovered, but we immediately realized the importance of it."

The screen then began cycling through the contents of the hard drive. There were technical diagrams, chemical components, crude sketches, mathematical equations, journal entries, all presented to Matt in a dazzling flash of holographic imagery.

"We don't know the exact specifics of what he was working on before he was killed, but as far as we can tell, he was on the brink of designing some type of pathogen. A synthesized biological weapon. One that, while relatively harmless to humans, would be devastating to the Wraith." Adderson paused again before continuing. "Matt, Rossiter believed this pathogen could destroy the Wraith and end the war."

Matt raised his eyebrows. "That's a helluva claim, sir."

"It is. And if true, it would imply he simply didn't have enough time to develop it any further." Adderson clicked his finger and a single image on the screen froze. He then pinched the air and the image zoomed in. "This was his final journal entry."

Matt leaned forward in his chair, squinting at the image on screen. Underneath the written entry was a series of chemical equations.

"Approximately one hour after he typed that entry, his entire facility was destroyed by an enemy strike. This facility was a remote, highly classified bio-defense unit near Papoose Lake. It was in the middle of the Nevada desert. There was no surrounding population for miles. The closest populated area was the Vegas ruins. Coincidence?"

Matt looked up at Adderson, still trying to process all of this. "Sir, are you saying the Wraith somehow knew what he was working on?"

"I'm saying *maybe*. Maybe they had a spy who managed to infiltrate his team. Hard to say."

"I'm sorry, sir, but— how exactly do I fit into all of this?"

"I want you to find him."

Matt was struggling to hide his confusion. "But— you just said he was killed during the invasion."

A tiny grin creeped into the corner of Adderson's mouth before there was a firm knock at the door. "Come in," Adderson commanded.

A young USC soldier entered, holding a small tablet. She placed it on the table in front of Matt, turned and abruptly left the room, closing the door behind her.

Adderson motioned for Matt to look at what was on the tablet screen.

He did.

On screen was a digital document marked: *CLASSIFIED. USC/NSC/CSOC EYES ONLY*.

"Matt, before we can talk any further I'm going to need you to sign that document."

Matt scanned the dense military legal-speak. "Oath Upon Inadvertent Exposure to Classified Data or Information?"

Adderson leaned back into his chair, folding his arms. "It's essentially a fancy way of saying - if you ever divulge any part of this conversation to anyone, you will be thrown into a military prison for life, without trial."

"Ah... shouldn't I have a lawyer look over this first?"

Adderson scoffed. "The President doesn't even have the clearance level needed to read that document. Matt, I'm not forcing you to sign it. You don't have to. But I'm afraid this will be where our conversation ends."

Matt looked back down at the screen, then sighed. He pressed his right thumb against the bottom of the screen. There was a chime, indicating his print signature was verified. He slid the tablet back over to Adderson.

"Thank you." Adderson then stood and began to slowly pace the room, thoughtfully considering how he was going to proceed. "Matt, since the USC launched its counter-strike initiative, I've been part of a joint program with the Office of Scientific Defense. The primary objective of this program was to develop the technology to travel back in time." Adderson paused for effect. "That technology, although very limited in its capability, is now fully operational."

There was silence from Matt. If he was baffled before, he was almost beside himself now.

"Before Rossiter was sent to Papoose Lake, he worked for Homeland Security at the National Bio-defense Analysis and Countermeasure Center in Maryland. He also had an apartment in Washington D.C. which he frequented. Matt, we want to send you back to D.C., forty-eight years before the first attack. We want you to find Dr. Rossiter and give him the contents of that drive."

Matt could barely form the words needed to respond. "I— I don't understand. Why?"

"Buy us some time. If we have that pathogen ready before the

Wraith arrive, we've already won the war. It could even prevent the war from happening."

"No, I mean— why me?"

"To this day, no USC soldier has ever escaped a Wraith enhancement facility, let alone rescue seven POWs. We've also never had a unit penetrate the Capital as deeply as you and your squad did. It's because of you, we've managed to learn a lot about their ground force chain of command. I can assure you, your combat record has been scrutinized more than any other candidate for this mission."

Matt sat there, his mind reeling with a million questions. "You want to send a soldier? Why not another scientist?"

"We already have."

Matt looked at Adderson with disbelief. "You've already sent people back?"

Adderson gave a firm nod. "There's a small team waiting for you in the year 2018. However, they're scientists more than they are soldiers, and this mission does require some significant... grunt."

Then, it dawned on Matt. "You want to kidnap him."

"That would be the most tactical strategy. You can't risk divulging any of this information in public. And under no circumstances can anyone know where you are from, or why you are there."

"What happens once I make contact?"

"Your team will debrief Dr. Rossiter and begin working with him. You'll also serve as mission security."

"How do you communicate with this team?"

"We don't," Adderson replied sharply.

"So, how do we all make it back?"

"You don't. It's a one-way ticket only, I'm afraid."

For a second, Matt thought he may actually pass out.

Adderson took his seat again. "I understand it's a lot to ask of you - especially when you've already given so much. But I need you to do it again. The whole of humanity needs you to do it again... I understand some men and women died under your command during your time on Epsilon?"

Matt immediately felt his stomach tighten. "Not some. I lost my entire squad, sir."

"I know how that feels. Believe me, I have grieved for every soldier I ever lost in battle... Matt, I can assure you, if you do this, none of their deaths will have been in vain. This could change the tide of the war completely."

"Sir, with all due respect, I just got home after a six-year tour. Now you're asking me to leave my family again. This time, forever?"

Adderson nodded solemnly.

Matt studied Adderson's eyes as they seared back at him. They were talking soldier to soldier, but there was no sense of empathy whatsoever in the tone of his voice. The mission was the only thing this man cared about. "You can't expect me to do this."

That response caused Adderson to bristle slightly in his seat. He was careful not to break composure. "If not for me, do it for the very same reasons you decided to join the USC after the Wraith slaughtered your wife. Do it for your daughter's future."

"And exactly what kind of future will that be - growing up without a mother or father? I'm sorry, sir, but I can't do it."

"You've seen it out there with your own eyes, son. We are *not* winning this war. Wraith numbers keep growing. For every battalion we take out, another three appear to take its place. Matt, this is it. This is our last roll of the dice."

Matt kept his eyes on the table and slowly shook his head. "To play God?"

"Maybe that's what it will take to save us. To prepare us for what's coming. Tell me, where was God when nine-million Portuguese were eradicated in a single afternoon? Or when the entire population of Delaware was reduced to a smoldering crater. You know what I'm saying is the truth, Matt. We can continue throwing bodies at this war and hope for the best, or we can do something to prevent it from ever happening."

And with that, Adderson abruptly grabbed the tablet, stood, and headed for the door. "Make no mistake, they *will* attack Earth again.

It's only a matter of time. Quite literally." He stopped short of the door, turning to face Matt again. "If you do this, there's still a chance your daughter can have a future. Perhaps a very bright one."

Matt didn't respond. His eyes just stayed fixed on the table, coiled with tension. The image of Dr. Rossiter flickered slightly on the screen, causing him to look up.

"I'll be back in one hour." Adderson opened the door and left.

The room suddenly fell silent, as if all the air was sucked out of it.

THIRTY

LYNETTE STOOD at the kitchen sink, washing some dishes under hot water, staring vacantly out the window in front of her.

The sun was setting over their field. It wasn't always this barren. It was once nearly two-hundred acres of green paddocks filled with livestock. Lynette thought back to how Jacob would take his Quad bike out on Saturday mornings to check on the cows. As a kid, Matt would always tag along, riding on the back with Clyde. He used to excitedly wave at Lynette each time they'd zip by the house on return trips to the bale shed. The thrum of Jacob's bike, along with Clyde barking always made her feel warm and content. It was only now, years later, she missed those sounds. Now, for the most part, the field was silent and lifeless.

Despite Matt's fondness for the farm, Lynette always knew her son would want to pursue a real career once he got older. She was pleasantly surprised when Matt broke the news he wanted to join law enforcement. In a small town with not a lot of job opportunities, it was a profession he could be proud of.

Jacob also knew Matt was only going to be interested in working with him on the farm for so long. With automated harvesters, and genetically modified food products widely used the world over, Jacob and Lynette were a dying breed. Nevertheless, as parents, they made sure their son developed an appreciation for working on the farm. If anything, it gave Matt a sense of duty and purpose. He also came to understand the value of an honest day's work. For Lynette and Jacob, that was good enough.

She snapped out of her daydream when she heard the distant thump of hypersonic rotors. She leaned over the sink and peered out the window, spotting a familiar object in the sky rapidly approaching the house.

Dishes clinked as she frantically wiped her soapy hands on her apron and hurried out towards the front door. "Jacob, get Ally! Come quickly!" Once again, Clyde started barking furiously at the sound of an incoming Helo. She rushed outside, the old screen door creaking shut behind her.

Jacob and Ally joined her on the front porch. "It's Daddy! He's back!" Ally took off like a rocket.

Jacob went to snatch her, but she was too quick. "Ally, wait!" He only just managed to stop Clyde from sprinting after her.

The Valor touched down.

Matt hoped out and began walking across the field, shielding his eyes from the swirling tornado of dust the powerful rotors had kicked up. He now wore a blue jumpsuit, which looked similar to the training suits NASA Astronauts might have once worn.

Matt ducked as the Valor took off again, banking low over the field, away from him.

Then, Ally met her father's arms.

"Which one is it?" said Ally, nestling her back against Matt's chest. They were both sitting on the rickety steps of the front porch, looking up at the brilliant night sky.

Matt took her tiny hand and raised it up to her eye-line, gently extending her index finger. "It's right on the tip of your finger. See it?"

Ally repositioned herself, squinting at the end of her finger. "Why is it so bright?"

"It's a much bigger sun than our own. They call it a Red Giant. But you know what? I like to think the real reason it's so bright, is because there are so many brave men and women there right now, protecting Earth, keeping us all safe down here."

Ally relaxed back into his arms, her green eyes still on Epsilon's star. "Grandma said they put you to sleep in a really cold box on the way home. What's it like?"

Matt chuckled. "You mean apart from being really cold? I don't remember all that much, but I know I dreamed a lot."

"About what?"

Matt was suddenly struck with the image of Pinehurst, sprawled out on the ground, bleeding profusely as he screamed for Matt to help him. He pinched his eyes shut in an attempt to expel the horrific imagery from his mind. Then, he kissed the top of Ally's head and stood. "Come on, little munchkin. It's time you went to bed."

"Munchkin? I'm not four anymore, dad."

"I know. I'm still getting used to that."

When they both turned to walk up the porch stairs, they saw Lynette swishing off down the hallway. She had been listening to them the entire time.

Matt knew why.

THIRTY-ONE

JACOB STOICALLY GLANCED up from his mug of tea as Matt entered the kitchen. Matt could tell his father had been alone, deep in thought for quite a while.

He took a seat opposite his father at the kitchen table.

"You want some tea?" Jacob asked.

"I'm fine, thanks."

They sat there, a moment of thick silence passing between them before Jacob finally revealed what was on his mind. "You have to tell her you're leaving."

Matt kept his eyes on the kitchen table and let out an exhausted sigh. "I can't break her heart like that, dad"

"She's already lost her mother. You'll never stop her heart from breaking. But you can at least give her a reason why you're leaving, even if it is a lie. Maybe then she won't grow up to resent you."

Matt studied the wedding band on his finger, his mind racing with a million thoughts. "Dad, if the Wrath attack us again, promise me you won't let Ally or Mom suffer. Not like Karen did."

Jacob looked at Matt with a hint of bewilderment and concern.

"Of course not. Matt, you have to stop blaming yourself for Karen's death."

"I wasn't there when she needed me, dad. If I was, perhaps she'd still be alive."

"Look, I know whatever it is you're doing is important, so I'm not even going to try and talk you out of it. But you have to learn to forgive yourself, Matt. You can't change what's already happened. You can't alter the past."

Matt met his father's eyes. "Maybe not. But I am going to try."

Ally was curled up under her pink sheets, sleeping peacefully when the bedroom door gently creaked open. Matt stood by the doorway, silhouetted by the faint light of dawn. He knelt by Ally's bed and gently put his hand on her arm.

She stirred, her eyes slowly opening on Matt. "Dad?" She propped herself up, rubbing her eyes. "What's going on?"

Matt struggled to answer, his chin was already starting to quiver.

Ally had never recalled seeing him upset like this, but somehow she knew he was leaving her again. "Where are you going?"

"Away, sweetheart. I've got something very important I need to do."

"When will you be back?" she asked, her frown deepening.

Matt couldn't look at her. He dropped his head, tears peppering the duvet. "I'm— I don't think I'm coming back this time, Al."

Ally began to tear. "Why? Why do you have to leave again? Why?"

"Ally... listen to me. I want you to know, I love you very much. I always will. And whatever happens in the future, don't ever be afraid, OK? Ever."

Ally started crying. The fragility of a little girl who had just realized she was about to lose her father forever was too much to bear.

She climbed out from her blankets to embrace Matt. "Why can't I come with you?"

That's when Matt lost it.

He sobbed heavily, a river of tears pouring from his eyes. He was hugging Ally so tight he thought she may pass out. But he didn't care. He just wanted to hold her for as long as possible and never let go. "I don't know how, but I'm going to find a way to get back to you, Al."

"You promise?"

"I promise. I'll always love you, Al... today, tomorrow, and forever."

THIRTY-TWO

THE MORNING SUN was just breaking over the horizon as Matt headed out across the field towards the Valor that was waiting for him.

None of the fear or anxiousness he felt when he left home for deployment, or the horrors he witnessed once he reached Epsilon, could have prepared him for this. Saying goodbye to his family forever was the hardest thing he had ever done. As he walked, each step felt as if it were weighed down by a ton of concrete.

Jacob, Lynette, and Ally stood on their front porch, watching Matt walk off, knowing it would be the last time they'd ever see him again. Jacob had to restrain Clyde by his collar with both hands. The dog sat there whimpering, itching to take off after Matt.

Before Matt climbed into the Valor, he turned to face them and put his hand up to wave goodbye.

Jacob and Lynette returned the gesture. Ally just stood there, her body shaking as she sobbed, paralyzed with sadness. Perhaps even anger.

Matt swallowed back the pain, turned and hopped aboard the craft.

As the Valor began to lift into the air and bank away, Matt never took his eyes off them.

Matt knelt in front of Karen's tombstone, gently brushing aside some dead leaves and straightening the most recent flower bouquet Lynette had left.

He thought about all the wonderful moments they had shared over the years, like the very first time they met. The first time they made love. Their close-knit wedding at a small church in Lawrenceburg, where it was so hot, Matt had struggled to slide the wedding ring onto Karen's swollen finger. The sheer joy of seeing Karen give birth. Ally's first words. Her first steps. Her first birthday. Matt would treasure these memories for the rest of his days.

He kissed his hand and pressed it against the epitaph inscribed into the marble.

Karen Michelle Wilson. 2022-2048. Beloved Daughter, Wife, and Mother.

Matt then rose to his feet, turned and walked off.

Adderson was waiting for him by the cemetery's wrought-iron gates.

THIRTY-THREE

THE VALOR SKIMMED low over the frigid waters of Shelikof Strait, heading towards Kodiak Island, two-hundred-and-fifty miles from the Alaskan mainland.

Matt looked out his passenger-side window. The icy water below was dark and glassy. If, for whatever reason, they were unlucky enough to have to ditch, the crew and passengers would be dead within minutes. He gripped his harness with white knuckles as the Valor suddenly banked hard and wide, buffeted by perilous cross-currents.

Then, a sprawling military base came into view on the edge of the island. It was partially embedded into the side of a glacial mountain, surrounded by a dense, snow-capped forest. Large antenna arrays and radio towers could be seen looming above the trees. The base itself was made up with clusters of white, bulbous-shaped buildings and hangars that looked like golf balls. A vast network of runways connected each section of the facility.

The Valor began its descent.

The Valor landed just outside the facilities main hangar. Adderson and Matt climbed out, accompanied by a small detail of Praetorians and support personnel.

They were greeted by Dr. Lucas Cosgrove and his team. Like many military and civilian scientists during the invasion, Cosgrove was scooped up from the private defense contracting and aerospace industries. By the time he reached his mid-forties, he had already become the USC's Lead Scientific Engineer and Special Access Programs Director. A coveted role many of his colleagues hated him for. Ten years on, he was considered one of the most vital cogs in the USC's labyrinthine war machine. Despite his brilliance, he also developed a reputation for being overly-fastidious, and at times, difficult to work with.

Adderson was first to shake Cosgrove's gloved hand. "Good to see you again, doctor," he said, his hot breath clouding around him.

"Likewise," Cosgrove replied. He then turned his attention to Matt. "Hello, Matt. It's good to finally meet you."

Matt nodded and shook his hand, trying hard not to show his chattering chin.

Cosgrove gently ushered Matt and Adderson towards the large hangar opening. "Come, I'll introduce you to the rest of my team once we get you underground. Matt, I want you to know, if there's anything you need while you're here, don't hesitate to ask."

"Thank you," Matt replied.

They followed Cosgrove and his team into the large hangar. It was filled with supplies, electrical equipment, and military hardware. A lot of it looked familiar to Matt.

Cosgrove spoke as if he was giving a museum tour. "This base was once a spy satellite tracking station. It was built during the Cold War years. A lot smaller than this originally, but since the invasion, we dramatically expanded it. It's now primarily a testing facility. We also liaise with other USC bases and research facilities around the world."

Matt noticed a large banner draped across the far end of the hangar. It was faded and tattered. The Latin motif of *Unitas Est Fortitas* could barely be read.

Adderson saw Matt curiously looking at it. He leaned in closer to him as they walked. "It says '*unity is strength*'. After the USC was formed, I figured we'd leave it up there. It's a nice reminder of what mankind can achieve when united for a common cause."

Cosgrove turned and signaled for them to stop.

Matt looked down and realized they were standing inside a large red circle that had been painted on the concrete floor.

Cosgrove waved to the USC troop sitting inside the small control module unit above them. "Watch your arms, ladies and gents."

There was a dull mechanical thud as the ground began to sink. A safety chain-link emerged, surrounding them as the huge disc-shaped platform began its descent underground.

THIRTY-FOUR

THERE WAS a heavy jolt as the platform touched down, causing Matt to lose his balance.

He also lost his ability to speak.

They were in an enormous underground space - part missile silo, part research laboratory. It bustled with activity, inhabited with a mixture of scientists and armed guards. A maze-like hodgepodge of work modules and cubicles filled the entire area. Most of the ventilation system was exposed, drooping down from the high ceiling like a rat's nest of wires. The muffled roar of several large power generators could be heard in the distance, each one the size of a small house.

Matt looked around in awe, his jaw slack. "My... god."

Cosgrove grinned. "Impressive, isn't it? We're now twenty-three stories underground. But you ain't seen nothing yet. Follow me."

Cosgrove led them down a starkly bland corridor which was stationed with armed guards every thirty feet or so.

Matt noticed these guards wore black uniforms which did not feature any insignia or emblems. They were not USC. Most likely some sort of private security apparatus. Since the invasion, there were now dozens of *unacknowledged* agencies scattered around the world, all vying for lucrative USC contracts to produce the next big breakthrough in defense technology. The residual effects of this war had created a new arms race between nations. However, the purpose was no longer to use these weapons against each other, but rather, a new common enemy.

They all stopped in front of a massive iron doorway that towered at least thirty-feet above them. It looked like a cross between a submarine hatch and a bank vault.

Cosgrove put his face up to the holographic control panel. A thin robotic arm extended from the wall, projecting a laser grid-pattern over his face as it scanned his eyes. There was a soft chime, followed by a green flash on the control panel as the iris scanner retracted back into the wall.

Then, there was a deep mechanical jolt from within the hatch as its internal locking mechanisms began to move.

Matt could feel the entire corridor vibrating. It immediately reminded him of a certain mission he once conducted on Epsilon, where he infiltrated an underground Wraith facility.

The giant hatch cracked open. Cosgrove motioned for them to follow him through.

It was another massive underground space, cored out of solid bedrock, part NASA mission control, part Hadron Collider. By terrestrial standards, this was a marvel in Geo-engineering and design. The superconductor centered in the middle looked like some type of enormous cannon. Coolant hissed from a tangled array of pipes and solenoid vents. Small teams of scientists, all wearing hard-hats and lab coats, manned the various consoles dotted around the superconductors base, working holographic screens and high-tech equipment. The temperature was also freezing cold.

Smirking with pride, Cosgrove turned to Matt, whose expression had descended into a state of pure and utter shock. "Welcome to The Emissary Program. Matt, this is the crown jewel of USC ingenuity. Yes, we've figured out how to traverse the gulf of deep space in little, to no time at all, but this — this is arguably our greatest achievement."

Matt took a moment to study the gigantic piece of machinery that towered over them. "You built a goddamn time machine?"

"Well, yes and no. Think of it as a giant particle collider. We charge it up and fire over nine-hundred-trillion proton collisions per second. That allows us to, very briefly, manipulate the fabric of space and time itself. We're essentially tapping into the quantum energy field which the universe is made up of, and using it as a transportation mechanism."

"And you want to put me inside this thing?" Matt said, still reeling with awe.

Still smiling, Cosgrove could see Matt's unease. "Rest assured, you won't be the first to enter it."

Matt snickered, shaking his head. "No offense, but somehow that doesn't fill me with much comfort."

Cosgrove adjusted his spectacles then continued. "Matt, there's a lot we need to do before you're even ready to climb in. You'll be in quarantine for the next three months. Let's get you rested up first and we can resume this tomorrow."

Matt turned to Adderson with a tense look. "I gave up everything I've ever known to do this. It better work."

Adderson returned the look. "It will. It has to."

The next morning, Matt found himself sitting in a sterile, featureless room. No windows, no visible ducting, just four tiled walls and a small air vent above him. He sat in a chair, which had already been placed in the middle of the room when he was escorted in an hour earlier by one of those mysterious, nondescript guards. There was a single pane of one-way glass in front of him. He figured someone had been watching him for the entire time he'd been sitting there. Maybe Cosgrove or Adderson. Maybe both.

The door clicked open and a man wearing a Hazmat suit entered, holding an ominous looking black case.

Straight away, Matt thought the worst. There was probably an array of injections he'd need to endure. Or perhaps some type of cross-examination to ensure he was at peak mental and physical condition.

The Hazmat man put the case on the corner table that was against the back wall. He clicked it open and pulled out an electric head shaver. He switched it on, moved over to Matt and began shaving his head.

Matt looked down at a thick clump of brown hair that fell into his lap and snickered to himself.

Cosgrove and Adderson were indeed standing in another room behind a sound-proof pane of one-way glass, watching him intently. Cosgrove leaned forward and spoke into the intercom panel next to him. "Matt, this is not for any sanitary reasons like it was on Epsilon. We're simply removing as much body hair as we can for the purpose of the Embryo."

Matt looked up at the one-way glass. "Embryo?"

THIRTY-FIVE

A BALD-HEADED Matt stood in front of a yellowish, pill-shaped capsule - *the Embryo*.

He softly pressed a finger into the rim of the capsule. When he pulled it out, there was a squishy, gelatinous substance on the tip of his finger. It smelled like toothpaste.

Matt was in another featureless room that was connected to a series of plexiglass cubicles. A small team of scientists could be seen working away in each one.

Cosgrove stood behind Matt as he examined the Embryo. "This is the capsule we'll encase you in. It will help protect your cellular structure as you go through time."

"This stuff reminds me of Curd," Matt said, grimacing at the very thought.

Cosgrove nodded with a grin. "It's very much like Curd, but a lot less smelly." Cosgrove then ushered Matt over to a medical gurney. "Hungry?"

Matt hopped up onto the gurney, laying on his back. "I was until *Curd* was mentioned."

Cosgrove chuckled as he wheeled over an intravenous drip.

"Now, over the course of the next three months, we'll need to lower your overall body mass. Starting from now, you'll be on a special liquid diet only. The lighter you are, the easier it will be for your body to travel back." Cosgrove tapped a vein in Matt's arm, rigging the cannula to an intravenous bag filled with dark green fluid. "However, a liquid diet cannot be at the expense of losing muscle mass. You're still going to need optimum strength if this mission is to be a success. So, we'll get you on a treadmill each day for a few hours, and we'll combine that with some weight training."

Matt could feel a cold sting traveling up his arm as the liquid began to course through his veins. He glanced over at the side table behind Cosgrove and saw an open file floating there. It contained profile pictures; three men and one woman. "Those are my teammates?" he asked.

Cosgrove nodded. "They are indeed. We'll brief you on them a little later."

"Assuming my team wasn't zapped onto the surface of the sun, how will they know when to intercept me?"

Cosgrove slipped off his disposable gloves and waved at the file. A series of icons appeared. He cycled through some, then with another wave of his hand, a large 3D topographical map of Washington State expanded before Matt. "This is Washington D.C., 2018. Geographically, not much has really changed since then." Cosgrove pointed to a particular area on the map. "This is where your team will be waiting for you."

Matt studied the map, his frown deepening. "You're putting me into a body of water?"

Cosgrove zoomed in on the map by pinching two fingers in the air. "The Potomac River to be exact. The human body was not built for something like time travel. Water will act as a natural buffer. More specifically, it will also help insulate your body from any impacts during the re-materialization process." There was a soft chime. Cosgrove looked down at his tablet and began tinkering with some read-outs. "Ah, good. Your biometric diagnosis is green. Looks like you're adapting well so far. How do you feel?"

Matt rolled his tongue around inside his mouth. "Fine, I guess. But there's this taste in my mouth - like burnt spinach or something."

A holographic display of Matt's entire digestive system appeared above Cosgrove's tablet. He smiled while continuing to cycle through various data read-outs. "That's the nutrients your body is now absorbing. There's a whole battery of stuff; glucose, amino acids, lipids, added dietary vitamins. Might take a while before you get used to it."

"I'm already dying for a good steak."

Cosgrove looked up at him. "Well, there will be some residual effects from this - which I stress are perfectly normal given the circumstances."

"Like what?" Matt said, showing some sign of concern.

"You'll be sick for a few days. It will be hard to digest solids for some time."

"Awesome. I can hardly wait," Matt replied in a deadpan tone.

"Oh, don't worry too much. Your team will help you recover. They've all been through it themselves."

Matt watched Cosgrove go back to his tablet data. "Any idea what it's going to feel like - going back in time?"

Cosgrove hesitated before responding. "Matt, I'm not going to lie. It will probably be the most intense pain you've ever felt. We're working with a very small window of opportunity here. Adderson wouldn't want me telling you this, but there's also a slight chance you may come out the other side... not entirely whole."

Matt propped himself up on one elbow, uncertain he heard Cosgrove correctly. "Whole? Um... what does *that* mean?"

Cosgrove put his tablet down and then leaned against the table, folding his arms. "Well, we create a tear in the fabric of space. Then, we basically shotgun you through it. The problem - is that the tear only stays open for one trillionth of a second. So, if it closes before your entire body slips through... well, whatever's left behind, stays here."

Cosgrove could see Matt was stunned at this. He smiled, slapping Matt's back in an effort to lighten the mood. "But rest assured, we're doing everything to ensure something like that doesn't happen. You're in good hands, Matt. Now, tomorrow we'll start giving you the first round of immunization doses. Nothing too dramatic. They're simply designed to cover a host of bacterial threats you may encounter once you go back. In the meantime, try and get some rest."

And with that, Cosgrove scooped up his tablet and exited the room, leaving Matt alone to contemplate his fate.

THIRTY-SIX

KAREN WAS startled awake by a jarring explosion.

She was certain it came from somewhere across the street, either from the Malone or Baer residences. It could have been either one of the propane tanks they recently had installed. Or, Karen thought with dread, the street was being bombed.

The loud explosion had also startled Ally. She began to squirm in her seat, whimpering softly between bubbles and hums, which Karen knew all too well were signs of increasing agitation.

Karen gave her a reassuring smile, then raised her right index finger to her mouth. "Ssshhh. We have to stay quiet, Al," she whispered.

When Ally groaned louder, Karen began to gently rock her seat. "Time to go sleepies again, honey," she said, almost pleadingly. "Time to go sleepies."

But Ally was now wide awake and restless.

"Ally, sweetie. Please. Not now. You've got to go back to sl—" Karen paused upon hearing a loud shatter of glass downstairs. It sounded like the living room window and the kitchen back door had been smashed simultaneously.

Then, Karen heard them.

It was unintelligible and garbled, but there were at least three voices talking in unison. It did not sound like English. It did not sound like any language or dialect Karen had ever heard before. She could also hear the stairs creaking.

One of them was heading upstairs.

Karen gasped and put a hand to her mouth.

Ally's whimpers had become cries. Karen knew the intruders would hear her any second, if they hadn't already. She had to somehow try and muffle the sound.

She fished out a pile of old clothes from a nearby cardboard box, then picked Ally up from her seat, kissed her forehead, and gently placed her inside the box, covering her over with a pile of clothes. Karen positioned the clothes in a way that ensured Ally still had plenty of air to breathe. But the moment everything went dark for Ally, she shrieked in protest.

"I'm so sorry, Al. I'll be back real soon, I promise," Karen whispered to her, pulling out the loaded Smith & Wesson revolver Matt kept in a small safe on the top shelf of their closet.

She then slowly emerged out from the closet, swishing across the carpet on her knees. Ally's muted cries had become a muffled wail as Karen gently shut the closet door behind her and rose to her feet, tiptoeing over to the bedroom door. Her hands were trembling so much, she could barely hold the gun while she opened the door.

Karen stepped into the hallway, floorboards creaking underneath her bare toes. She could hear the intruders still communicating among themselves. She craned her neck over the staircase railing, careful not to make a sound.

Below, inhuman shadows churned and shifted. Whatever was down there, was ransacking the house.

She gingerly backed away, struggling to hold back tears. She was beyond terrified, her heart firmly stuck in her throat. When she heard a floorboard creak behind her, she spun around to see a Wraith soldier standing at the far end of the hallway, watching her curiously.

She tried to scream, but nothing came out.

The Wraith calmly took off its insidious-looking helmet and moved towards her, a malicious grin forming across its grey lips as it unsheathed a large jagged blade from a scabbard on its back.

This one was going to have its way with her. Slowly.

Karen found her scream and fired the revolver.

THIRTY-SEVEN

MATT SHOT UPRIGHT IN BED, gasping for air. "Karen! No!!!"

It took him a moment to realize he'd just had another terrible nightmare. He looked around his darkened room then down at his hairless chest, which was glossed in cold sweat. He breathed in deep and slow before laying down again. This was a breathing procedure he did in order to try and calm himself, as the nightmares were getting more frequent and more vividly intense since he arrived back on Earth. He never knew exactly what happened during Karen's last moments, but he had a pretty good idea. It was something he tried not to think about too much, but since being quarantined at this base, underground and without proper sunlight once again, he couldn't help it.

Matt clicked his fingers and a small reading lamp above him turned on. He sat upright again and reached for the water jug beside his bed. Realizing how parched he was, he chugged the whole thing down in a few gulps. As he placed the jug back, his eyes landed on the hard-copy photo he had stuck to the side of his bed-side table.

It was an old photo Jacob gave him the morning he left to undertake this mission. In the photo, Matt, a very pregnant Karen, Jacob, and Lynette were all huddled together outside a restaurant. It was taken at a family lunch in downtown Frankfort, roughly one year before the invasion.

Matt gently lifted up the photo to see Jacob had handwritten something on the back of it in pen.

Good luck, Matt. We will always love you. - Mom, Dad, Karen, and Ally.

Matt studied the photo for a long time. Along with his wedding ring that Cosgrove took and sealed in something resembling an evidence bag, this photo was now essentially an artifact - the only proof connecting Matt to his previous life. Cosgrove was quick to inform Matt he wasn't authorized to take anything back in time with him for any reason. If any inorganic object or material was not properly insulated, the superconductor could malfunction. If the superconductor did malfunction during the de-materialization process, Matt could be incinerated, or worse, marooned in some alternate dimension. So, Matt decided he was going to memorize every pixel of detail in this photo. He would ingrain it into his memory so deeply, it would be virtually impossible for him to ever forget it.

He rolled back over to face the ceiling, still in deep thought. It would be three months tomorrow since he first arrived and began training for this mission. And while he still struggled with the pain of knowing he would never lay eyes on his family again, he also couldn't help but wonder what the past held for him. A new life awaited, and with it, the promise of a new future.

Matt jumped up from his bed and threw on a hoodie and a pair of sweatpants. He was wide awake now, so the only thing that would help him get back to sleep was his regular late-night jog around the base.

Matt came up on his final lap around the upper balcony that overlooked the superconductor and broke into a hard sprint.

The guards all knew Matt's nightly routine but still watched him with eagle-eyes regardless.

As Matt closed out the final few meters, he checked the clock display above him. For the third time in two weeks he had beaten his own record. He took a breather against the railing, sucking the cool artificial air into his lungs as sweat dripped from his bald head. He was by far in the best shape he'd ever been in, but tonight he pushed himself that extra bit harder. He looked over at the two guards standing across from him and gave them a nod.

They both returned it with a grin. Matt heard a couple of the guards had been betting on his running times, and it looked like these two just made some money.

Matt turned his attention to the superconductor humming away underneath him.

To stand high above it with a perfect top-down view was always impressive. He had looked at this piece of machinery every day and night for the past three months, and he still marveled at the intricate elegance of its design. However, there was also something ominous about it - a feeling that, despite what the Wraith had forced the USC to do, this machine should never have been built to begin with.

Matt glanced up at the clock display again.

Six hours left until departure.

THIRTY-EIGHT

ZERO HOUR. Intense floodlights illuminated the superconductor. Outside the isolation chamber, an army of tech teams, engineers, and support personnel teemed around their terminals like ants, examining the vast array of diagnostic data and pre-launch read-outs.

Matt entered the isolation chamber surrounding the superconductor, stepping up onto a ringed tier. He was barefoot, wearing something that resembled a hospital gown.

Wearing hazmat suits with sterilized breathing filters over their mouths, Adderson and Cosgrove followed behind him. They walked slow as if they were both underwater, their breath hissing with each step.

For the last time, Matt looked up with dread at the massive machine that towered before him, still struggling to comprehend how this thing could possibly work.

There was an eerie uniformity to the low hum it was emitting. Girders rattled, circuitry hummed, and metal moaned under the enormous pressure being produced inside. Matt could feel the entire chamber vibrating. The Embryo pod itself was connected to the superconductor by an unfathomable tangle of multi-colored wires and heavy feeder cables. Once Matt was sealed inside the pod, it would be inserted into the superconductors core, much like a round being loaded into the chamber of a revolver.

Cosgrove carefully opened the clamshell pod that housed the Embryo. Vapor hissed as the cover lifted, cascading across the floor to where Matt stood. It felt cold as it swirled around his legs. He turned around to take one final look at this timeline.

Cosgrove gave him an earnest nod. "Good luck, Matt. And thank you."

Adderson saluted him. "Godspeed. We're counting on you."

Matt returned the salute to Adderson, gave Cosgrove a respectful nod, then watched them turn and leave the chamber. Once they had exited into an observation module, he disrobed, naked as the day he was born.

He climbed into the Embryo pod, curling into a fetal position while sinking into the cold, gelatinous substance. There was a sharp hiss of air being sucked out as the clamshell cover sealed shut over him. It was claustrophobic and sterile - a little more spacious than a coffin. Matt could barely move, encased in the thick Embryo goo. He closed his eyes, his breathing intensifying when he felt a sudden jolt of movement. The soft hum had morphed into a loud hydraulic whine. Matt knew it was the Embryo pod inserting itself into the superconductors core. He kept his eyes pinched tight, feeling the tiny hairs on his body stiffen, giving him goosebumps. The air felt electrically charged, and the hydraulic whine quickly became a deafening mechanical pounding. Matt dared to open his eyes. He immediately regretted it.

Everything around him was warping like a fish-eye lens.

"Oooohhh, god..." he yelled.

The mechanical pounding continued until it flat-lined into a static squeal. At that moment, Matt's entire existence was enveloped by a searing white light.

THIRTY-NINE

THE TWO HOODED men huddled from the freezing cold in their small rowboat as they paddled along the calm, icy waters of the Potomac River, their hot breath pluming into the night sky.

Although they were only twenty miles southwest of downtown D.C., this part of the Potomac felt rural and deserted, with the heavily wooded shoreline effortlessly masking all signs of life.

Dario Bollard stopped rowing. He pulled out the compass from his fur-lined Parka, checking the longitude and latitude coordinates he had scribbled on a piece of paper. He checked his watch before blowing breath into his cupped hands. Bollard was only in his early thirties, yet his dark eyes betrayed an intelligence that was well beyond his years. He looked up at his companion. "This is it. Now we wait."

The other man sitting across from him was Michael Wu. Like Bollard, Wu was only in his early thirties, and he too looked like a man who had lived beyond his age. The jagged scar that trailed down his left cheek also made him look slightly thuggish. Wu switched on his flashlight and panned it across the still dark water underneath them. "They never tell you how cold it's going to be down there."

Bollard also craned over the edge of the boat, scanning the freezing water for any sign of movement. "He'll be fine. Assuming it didn't close on him before he went through."

Then, there was a green flash of light directly underneath their boat, like some type of strange electrical discharge. It was followed by a huge air bubble that rose to the surface and popped.

Bollard grabbed the oars and rowed a little to the left of the bubbling green water. Wu leaned over the edge of the boat, dangling his arms into the frigid water. "Here he comes."

A column of water shot high into the air as a massive clump of Embryo belched through the surface, violently ejecting Matt out before sinking. He hit the water with a loud slap, still encased in yellow goo.

"Grab him! Quickly!" barked Bollard.

Wu grabbed the other oar and stretched it out for Matt.

Matt was semi-conscious, his arms flailed around until one hit the oar. He gasped for air, struggling to grip the oar with his slippery hands. He began to sink, hacking water. "Help—Help me— "

Wu managed to get close enough to latch his hands underneath Matt's armpits, hauling him up into the boat, careful not to capsize. Bollard stood and assisted. All the commotion was causing the boat to rock wildly.

Matt collapsed into the middle of the small boat, his body convulsing as he vomited up a mix of brackish water and Embryo residue.

Wu clicked open a supply case, pulling out a thick blanket and some thermal mylar foil, draping them around Matt's shivering shoulders. "Just relax. We've got you. Deep breaths now."

Matt's eyes sluggishly opened on Bollard, his purple lips clenched tight, teeth chattering like dinner plates.

Bollard was grinning back at him, knowing exactly what he was experiencing. "Congrats, you made it through. Welcome to 2018, Matt."

At that moment, Matt passed out.

FORTY

MATT DROVE the patrol car like a madman, unloading his horn, weaving around the gridlock of vehicles in front of him. "Get outta the way! Move!"

The wail of the police siren was to no avail - outside was absolute chaos and pandemonium.

Matt slammed on the brakes, screeching up behind a burning vehicle that sat lopsided on the rim of a huge blast crater.

Up ahead, he could see dozens of charred vehicles strewn across both lanes, passengers taken completely by surprise, flash-heated bodies fixed into horrific poses, like some form of instant rigor mortis. There was no way to break through and continue driving, and even if he could, there was no way he could drive over the smoking rubble of asphalt that was once Capital Avenue. He was going to have to get out and walk back to Harrisonville. Maybe he would be lucky enough to hitch a ride with another patrol car or find an undamaged vehicle along the way that had been abandoned.

Either way, he needed to get home to Karen and Ally, fast.

Matt tried the comms device on his wrist again, but it still gave him nothing but garbled static. Everything was down. He opened his *door and got out, cursing himself for not answering Karen's call earlier that day when he had the chance. An acrid mix of smoke and burning fuel assaulted him as he took in the carnage unfolding.*

Fires raged from battered storefronts on both sides of Capital Avenue, their flames billowing out onto the road. Pockets of black smoke churned and twisted up over the horizon as far as the eye could see. The State Capitol building was nothing but a smoldering ruin.

All around him, people were screaming and running for their lives in every direction. Some people hid in shops and what remained of government buildings. Some people stood there in the middle of the street, shellshocked and unable to process what was taking place.

Matt looked up as a huge shadow suddenly washed over the street. He stared with disbelief, unable to even form the words to speak.

An enormous Wraith battleship loomed overhead, eclipsing the sun like an apocalyptic blight.

FORTY-ONE

MATT'S EYELIDS slowly peeled open. Everything was a blur.

He could tell he was in a small, dimly lit room of some kind, curled up on a lumpy mattress. It was warm. Almost too warm. He tried moving his legs. That hurt.

A thick shadow washed over him, instinctively causing him to roll onto his back. He clenched his jaw through the pain of sudden movement. As he wiped some embryo crust from his red-raw eyes, they managed to focus a little better. But not much.

There were four figures standing by his bed. He recognized two of them; Bollard and Wu. But the others were too blurry to make out. He had read the dossier on his team before he left, so he assumed the other two people were Issac Gibbons, and Rhea Vega.

"Where am I?" Matt asked in a croaky voice.

"Safe house."

Matt vaguely recognized Wu's voice.

Wu approached the bed, holding something out for Matt to take. "Here, drink this. You'll need to rehydrate yourself."

Matt reached for the plastic cup. It felt as if his bones were on fire as he struggled to hold the cup, his jittery hands causing the liquid inside to splash all over his lap. It was at that moment he realized was still naked. He drank deeply, his throat severely parched. The liquid tasted mildly sweet, which he assumed was some type of Lucozsade. He could feel the relief it gave as he drained the rest of the cup. "Thank you," he said, in a slightly less croaky voice.

Rhea stepped forward with a small stack of fresh blankets. She was in her late twenties, Hispanic, and much more attractive than Matt remembered from her dossier profile. Her olive skin and tousled black hair gave her a somewhat earthy, natural look. She flung one of the blankets over Matt, her expression unreadable. "You'll feel like shit for the next few days, but it'll pass," she said.

Matt picked up the drawl in her accent. It wasn't over-the-top Southern belle, the vowels were more rounded, but there definitely was a slight musicality to it. Matt thought it sounded nice, and in a way, comforting.

The oldest of the group, Gibbons, placed a white paper bag on the end of the bed. Matt remembered his age was forty-seven, but his grey stubble made him look slightly older. He was African-American, with muscular broad shoulders that seemed at odds with his bookish demeanor. Matt had been warned by Adderson that Gibbons was fiercely intelligent and could be thorny on the best of days. He was also in command of this mission. "We took the liberty of getting you some clothes," he said in a rather glib tone. "They should fit you. Let me know if they don't."

Matt noticed Gibbons was missing his left arm, with his shirt folded neatly over the stump of his elbow. Matt immediately remembered what Cosgrove said about going through whole and begun to frantically check himself over to see if all his limbs were intact.

"Relax. You're good. I lost it during the invasion."

Matt looked up at Gibbons, feeling like a complete idiot. "I'm sorry— that wasn't in your file."

"It was, but I had them remove it. Figured it wasn't applicable."

Gibbons motioned to the bag at the end of the bed. "Embryo residue can stain the skin of it's not cleaned off within twenty-four hours. Mr. Bollard here will help you shower and dress. We'll debrief you once you've freshened up."

And with that, everyone except Bollard turned and left the room.

FORTY-TWO

BOLLARD HELD Matt upright as they entered the kitchen. He walked with a slight limp, still not entirely stable on his feet. Every muscle in his body hurt. It felt like they hadn't been used in years - like he was discovering them painfully for the very first time. "Cosgrove wasn't kidding when he said there'd be some negative effects on the body," he grumbled to Bollard, wincing as he took another step. He was dressed in the clothes provided by Gibbons; a pair of jeans, T-shirt, and a brown leather jacket. He thought they felt rather coarse and heavy compared to the fabrics he was used to in the future.

The rest of his team sat at a small kitchen table, watching him while they idly nursed mugs of coffee.

Matt gave them a polite nod and joined them, allowing Bollard to gently guide him into the chair. "Thanks," he said, his eyes drifting around the apartment to take in the visible squalor.

The first thing he spotted was the tower of dirty plates that arced out of the kitchen sink. There was also a small mountain of empty pizza and take-out boxes in the corner of the living room.

The drawn curtains hung like tattered rags, bathing the apartment in a murky yellow light, which reminded him of Epsilon's sickly-colored sky. The fixtures looked old, even for this time, and the pocked walls were grimy, with dark smears of mold bubbling up through the wallpaper in some corners.

This *safe house* was a total fucking dump.

Matt's eyes landed on the empty coffee mug in front of him. Even that looked a little grimy. "So this is 2018, huh?"

Gibbons' flinty eyes fixed on Matt. "I think it might be a good idea for us all to do a quick introduction. It'll also help refresh our memories on what each of us is tasked with... I'll start. I'm an Epidemiologist. Or at least I was. Before the war, I worked at Johns Hopkins Hospital in Baltimore, analyzing disease and infection control in populated areas. I'm going to assist Dr. Rossiter in the development and incubation process." Gibbons shifted his gaze to Bollard.

"Um... Dario Bollard. I work in Cytology. Basically, I study cell biology. Before the war, I worked for the Department of Defense out of the Walter Reed Medical Center in Bethesda. I'll be helping both Dr. Rossiter and Dr. Gibbons."

Rhea took a swig of her coffee and leaned back in her chair. "Yeah, I was a Medical officer for the CDC in Atlanta. I mainly worked in the public health field, dealing with non-governmental organizations. I'm going to help ya'll acquire and set-up the lab equipment needed to pull this off... Oh, I also spent some time as a Combat Medic in the USC after the shit hit the proverbial fan. Southern Corps. Was lucky enough to never get deployed off-world."

Wu raised his hand, gave Matt a nod. "Michael Wu. Systems Integrity Engineer, specializing in Architectural Synthesis. During the war, I was an interface designer for the USC. A lot of the HUD read-outs in your helmet were my idea." Wu reached into his jacket and pulled out a smartphone, holding it up for Matt to see. "Now I work with whatever I can. The software architecture on these devices can be a little rudimentary compared to what I'm used to, but I'm here to make sure we don't run into any unforeseeable tech problems."

Matt nodded back, taking a moment to absorb everything said. It was his turn. He cleared his throat and straightened in his chair. "OK... um... wow, everyone's a doctor or a scientist. I feel so inadequate."

"And why's that?" asked Gibbons, his tone laced with slight annoyance.

"Well, clearly you're all very... guess I'm really nothing more than a hired goon," he said with a tired smile. "I'm just here to help you guys with all the ugly stuff."

Gibbons leaned forward, annoyance now clearly etched into his creased brow. "Mr. Reeves, I want to make something absolutely clear. This may be a military operation in need of a *grunt* such as yourself, but I'm in command here. Am I understood?"

"Of course," Matt replied. He sensed Gibbons did not seem entirely satisfied with his response. "Apologies, I got home from a six-year tour on Epsilon before Adderson and Cosgorve told me I'd never see my family again. It's going to take me a while to deal with that," he added.

Gibbons shrugged. "You volunteered for this mission, correct?"

"I did. But that's not the point I'm trying to make."

"Then please, arrive at the point," said Gibbons dryly.

Matt wondered if Gibbons was intentionally goading him to evoke some kind of reaction. Maybe it was an attempt to expose a weakness or flaw. Some form of collateral that Gibbons could use against him if the need ever arose. Regardless, Matt maintained his poker-face. "Whatever's waiting out there— a lot of it will be completely alien to me. All of this. Everything. I'm a fish out of water."

"We all are," Gibbons replied.

"I know. And I can only imagine what you all felt when you first got here..." Matt met Gibbon's eyes before continuing. "Look, I was just trying to make light of our situation. Forgive me for cracking a little joke."

Gibbons studied him intensely for a moment, then deflated back into his chair. "I'm afraid jokes are a luxury we can't afford, Mr. Reeves. Must I reiterate the importance of what we're actually doing here?"

"No need. I'm well aware, sir."

"I hope so. I really do. Because we are attempting to alter the course of human history. We've got one chance to get this right. We cannot afford to make a single mistake."

Matt gave Gibbons a respectful nod. He wasn't here to cause friction with his teammates, especially not this early into the mission.

Gibbons drained his coffee mug and stood. "I'm going out to get some things. You should try and get acquainted with each other while I'm gone." Gibbons' eyes locked on Matt. "Maybe crack a few jokes." He then turned and abruptly exited the kitchen.

Matt watched him leave, waiting to hear the front door open and close. He then turned to the others with a wry smirk. "He seems like a fun guy."

Wu, Bollard, and Rhea chuckled in unison. Matt felt the lingering tension in the room immediately dissipate.

"Yeah, he's a bit of a hard-ass. But he's okay once you get used to him," said Bollard. "The war was really tough on him. He lost everything. From what I heard, his family was hiding in a basement, nearly starved to death when they were discovered by a Wraith patrol. His wife and four kids— all slaughtered right in front of him."

"They cut off his arm and left him there to bleed out," said Rhea. "But he didn't. Somehow, he survived. He kept going."

"Jesus," Matt said, his expression darkening as his own painful memories began to calcify in his mind. "Guess that explains a lot."

"Yep. This mission— in many ways it's consumed him," said Bollard. "Every afternoon he goes and sits in a park at the end of the street and thinks about what he has to do. He rarely sleeps either. Some nights he spends hours just trawling over his notes. I can see why Adderson put him in command. He's dedicated."

Rhea drained her mug. "You were a cop before the war?"

Matt gave her a taut nod. "Shelbyville P.D., Kentucky."

"What was that like?" she asked.

"Before the invasion? A little slow."

Rhea smiled.

"Tell me more about the data they recovered in Nevada," Matt said.

"Nothing much to say, except that Dr. Rossiter may have stumbled across the most important weapon since the creation of the atomic bomb," Bollard replied.

"Stumbled across is hardly the words I'd use. More like, *designed*," Rhea said, heading into the kitchen to refill her coffee mug. "He was on the verge of giving us a weapon the Wraith would never be able to defend themselves against." She returned with the entire coffee pot and placed it in the middle of the table on a large coaster.

Matt reached over and filled his empty mug.

"Drinking coffee won't do you any favors while you're still recovering," said Rhea. "It'll dehydrate you again."

Matt ignored her and filled his mug to the brim. "Sorry, but I can't function without my daily caffeine hit."

Rhea shrugged, taking a sip of her own mug. "Don't say I didn't warn you."

Matt gingerly took a sip and grimaced. "Oh— that's fucking horrible. Tastes like soapy water."

Wu and Bollard burst out laughing.

Rhea grinned with amusement. "Instant coffee, 2018. Straight up."

Wu watched Matt take another sip and shook his head. "I don't know, man. Sometimes I can't help but think all of this could be a complete waste of time."

"Annihilating the Wraith and preventing the invasion? Hardly a waste of time, I'd say," Rhea quipped.

"And what if we fail?" said Wu.

Rhea shrugged. "Then we fail. But at least we tried."

"So we just end up being nothing more than stranded tourists, with no way of ever getting back home?"

"We're already that, Wu," Rhea said. "Not being able to ever make it back home to our loved ones... we knew that was the sacrifice we'd be making before we signed up."

Matt placed his elbows on the table and leaned forward. "But, we don't know that for sure, right?"

Wu turned to Matt. "What do you mean?"

"I mean, it's all theoretical. All of this. We don't know for certain that we can't make it back home."

Rhea let out a cynical huff. "Ah, yeah, pretty sure this is a done-deal, Matt. There's no going forward in time, unless you can somehow build a machine like the one that sent us here. Good luck with that."

"But we still don't know if any of this will work. Adderson and Cosgrove are just hoping it does."

"That's exactly my point, though," said Wu. "We don't know shit. The fact that we're here now, altering the past— Rossiter could wake up tomorrow and get hit by a bus on the way to work. Then what?"

"Then, we are well and truly fucked," Rhea replied.

"But that's not going to happen," said Matt.

Wu looked at Rhea and Bollard incredulously, then back to Matt. "And why's that?" he half-snickered.

"Because we won't allow it to. We have to make this work. We don't have a choice."

Wu ran a hand through his jet-black hair. "If you say so. Hey, I won't say no to a little optimism."

Matt took another swig of his coffee. It still felt hard to swallow liquids, but he needed to wake up, and caffeine, no matter how horrid it tasted, was the only thing that would do the job. "This pathogen. What is it?"

"Before the Wraith came here, they knew everything about us," Rhea said. "They ensured their immune systems could withstand any natural biological threats we had. But this also meant that every single Wraith unit had to be given an array of various antibodies and medications, just to be able to handle our germs on the surface each day. We knew their bodies were as fragile as ours, but until we were able to fight back, it was their technology that gave them the advantage over us. However, what Rossiter discovered, is that there are two types of lymphocytes and leukocytes in the Wraith's blood system - and neither can produce the necessary cells required to defend against disease or bacteria. So, Rossiter went ahead and designed a pathogen that would be so devastating to their immune system, no amount of antibodies would ever be able to combat it. We're talking *Plague* 2.0. We're talking about something, that if contagious, could eradicate them within months. Possibly sooner."

"But there's going to be millions of them arriving here," said Matt. "And that's not counting the billions already on Epsilon."

"And that's the catch," Bollard said, clicking his fingers to emphasize his point. "In addition to Rossiter recreating the pathogen, he's also going to need to figure out how we can deliver a mass infection once they get here. He'll need to design some sort of payload system the USC can eventually take with them to Epsilon."

Matt took a moment to take all of that in, his mind racing. "And this pathogen— it's completely harmless to humans?"

"If Rossiter creates it exactly how he did in the future— yep, completely harmless."

"But how can you expect him to create something he hasn't even thought of yet?"

Before anyone could answer that question, there was the abrupt sound of the front door closing shut.

They all turned to see Gibbons walking in holding a Trader Joe's shopping bag. "That's simple. We give him the contents of his journal. However, there is one major problem he'll have to overcome."

"Which is?" Matt asked.

"In the future, he had an abundance of microbe samples from Epsilon, as well as Wraith specimens he could use as test hosts."

"So how will he overcome not having those now?"

That question hung heavy in the air before Gibbons replied. "Improvisation." Then, Gibbons brushed past them and headed to the kitchen sink, placing the bag on the bench. It was filled with fruit and vegetables.

He pulled out a smaller bag of fresh grapes, broke off a handful and rinsed them under the tap, all with his one hand. He shoved a few into his mouth, chewing greedily as he turned to face everyone at the table. "Dr. Rossiter is only twenty-six now, but he's already considered to be brilliant. That's why the Department of Defense snapped him up after he graduated from MIT. Right now, he's heading up a small research lab, mainly working on prevention protocols in cooperation with the CDC and some other Federal agencies. But he also holds a top-secret clearance level, so we suspect he's already involved in at least one classified project. Possibly more. And they most likely all revolve around bio-defense and viral warfare." Gibbons shoved another fistful of grapes into his mouth before continuing. "Mr Wu, would you care to show Mr. Reeves?"

"Sure." Wu held out a small silver chain that was draped around his neck. On the end of it was a tiny pill-shaped pod.

Matt immediately recognized it as a holofile.

Wu tucked it back down into his shirt. "Contains all of Rossiter's data, including his journal entries." He then placed a small, one terabyte flashdrive on the table. "It was also an absolute bitch to transfer over to this flashdrive."

"What the hell is a flashdrive?" asked Matt, as he leaned forward to get a better look at it.

Wu pulled off the protective cap, revealing the USB connector. "Universal Serial Bus. There's a few things you'll have to get used to here."

Wu then hopped up and grabbed the sleek notebook that was sitting lopsided on the arm of the sofa. There was a slim charging cord connected to a power socket in the wall. He pulled it out and returned to the kitchen. As he took his seat, he slid the notebook across the table to Matt.

Matt gingerly lifted the screen. "Feels so clunky."

Wu nodded in agreement. "Yeah, it can be slow too. But at least they have good wireless connections here. Mostly runs off a fiber backbone. Anyway, it took me days to convert the raw data into a readable format. I've tested it on several devices. Rossiter shouldn't have any problems accessing it."

"Shouldn't have?"

Wu turned to Gibbons, who was looking at him with an arched eyebrow while chewing his grapes.

Wu corrected himself. "Won't have, sir."

Matt gently closed the notebook's screen and looked up at Wu with slight bewilderment. "You brought the holofile with you?"

Wu nodded. He knew where Matt was going with this.

"Where'd you keep it?"

"You don't wanna know, man."

FORTY-THREE

THIS STRETCH of the Potomac River was still as a millpond. A thick blanket of fog hung over it, stretching all the way to the shoreline, curling around brittle tree stumps like some otherworldly miasma.

The gnarled wooden jetty that protruded out from the fog displayed an old sign promoting the wonderful fishing piers and nature trails of Piscataway Park, located on the tip of Accokeek, Maryland.

The tall man walked along the jetty, his footsteps calm and measured like they always were. Here, he was also known as *Cromwell*. The black Fedora hat he wore only accentuated his grim features, doing very little to conceal the coldness of his pale-blue eyes, and the pronounced jawline that was attached to the knotted sinew of his gaunt cheekbones.

As he walked, Cromwell kept his gloved hands buried deep within each pocket of his thick overcoat. Cromwell wanted Earth badly, but no Wraith cared much for the cold temperatures it could reach during the winter months, and this was the chilliest March

Cromwell cared to remember since he arrived here. He wondered if it would ever be possible to fully acclimatize.

He stopped walking, just shy of the jetty's edge, noticing something in front of him.

It was a smear of Embryo residue.

He bent down, pulled a glove off one of his hands and gently touched it, bringing his long fingers up to his sullen eyes so he could examine it closer.

He knew exactly what it was.

As he rubbed his fingers together, the skin tone around the tip of his fingers changed to a pale-gray. The residue had rubbed off part of the foundation make-up that was caked over his hands. Applying it each day with his contact lenses took hours, but it was the only way he could blend in without raising any suspicion. He wiped the yellowish substance off the tip of his fingers with a handkerchief, then slipped his leather glove back on. As he stood, something else caught his attention.

There was a wooden rowboat gently rocking against the shore, a few meters from the base of the jetty. It had been set alight and was now nothing but a blackened husk.

Cromwell knew they had sent Matt back.

FORTY-FOUR

MATT GRIPPED his sidearm with white knuckles, cautiously stepping through what remained of the front door to his home.

The interior of the house looked like it had been caught in a tornado. Family pictures dangled from shattered frames, tables had been flipped, glass cabinets sat lopsided and smashed.

"Karen?" Matt said with a tense hush.

No answer.

He began to frantically check every corner of the living room, making sure either Karen or Ally were not buried under a pile of upturned furniture. "Karen? Honey, you here?"

Still no answer.

He entered the hallway, broken glass crunching under each footstep as he edged towards the staircase that led up to the second-floor. He moved up the stairs slowly, gun raised, footsteps giving off a slight creak of wood. As his eyes came level with the second-floor landing, he saw her.

Karen's body was face-down in a puddle of dried blood, which had caked the floorboards in a thick, crimson sludge. Her lower torso was twisted in a sickening, unnatural pose. She had died violently.

"Karen! No!" Matt wailed hoarsely, as he scrambled up the stairs to reach her.

Sobbing heavily, he gently rolled her broken body over to see her face. That's when his legs buckled, and he collapsed next to her in a heap.

Matt was completely unaware of the gravely wounded Wraith soldier that sat slumped against a fallen side-table at the opposite end of the hallway, watching him while it clung to the last remnants of life. Black blood inched down through the intricate rivets of the Wraith's chest armor. The shot Karen managed to squeeze off before she was attacked had found its mark, the round punching directly through its exposed neck.

The soft gargle it gave when it coughed on some blood caused Matt to pause his weeping. He raised his head and looked around, his face was a rictus of pain and anguish, but his wet, red-raw eyes still bristled with alertness.

The wounded Wraith soldier met Matt's gaze and held it.

There was a brief pause from Matt, but the shock of what he was looking at was quickly overridden by searing rage. As he rose to his feet, he unleashed a gut-wrenching scream and rushed down the hallway.

The Wraith grunted with pain as Matt began belting it with a flurry of fists. The blows were relentless and brutal. Matt was frothing at the mouth like some rabid animal. Then, he collapsed onto his ass from the exhaustion of his outburst, his knuckles reduced to minced meat.

The dead Wraith's face was nothing but a battered pulp of bashed gore. Its entire lower mandible had been shattered, with many of its teeth mashed down into what remained of the oral cavity.

Matt sat hunched on the floor, struggling to put some air into his lungs, tears streaming from his eyes as they dripped onto his lacerated knuckles.

And that's when he heard it.

He struggled to listen. His heart was still pounding loudly in his ears, but he was certain he knew what that sound was.

There it was again.
It was coming from the master bedroom.
Ally's muffled cry.

FORTY-FIVE

MATT'S EYES SNAPPED OPEN. Rarely did a night pass now without him having to endure some horrific memory of Karen's death. He was starting to fear sleep altogether.

He rolled over and sat up on the edge of the bed, wiping away the beads of sweat peppered across his forehead. His bare chest, and the shorts he was wearing were also drenched. The sun was still a few hours from rising, but the room was stiflingly humid. He needed to cool off.

There was a small window in front of him, so he slid off the bed and walked over to it, cracking it open ajar to be greeted by a brisk draft. It was refreshing. He breathed in the chilly air and took a seat on the window-ledge, surveying the deserted street outside.

The apartment was nestled between Capitol Hill and Lincoln Park, and from this angle, Matt could just make out the U.S. Capitol building, its white dome, gleaming under the pre-dawn sky. Although their apartment was crummy and neglected, the neighborhood itself was leafy and somewhat affluent.

Matt surveyed the skyline with the fascination of a tourist. He had visited Washington D.C. once before, during a school trip when he was fourteen. But even with its historical landmarks, this time in America felt completely surreal to him - like he was simply a passenger observing another civilization from a distance. As he looked out over the city, he wondered about the millions of people, many of them politicians and public servants, many of them with families, completely unaware of what was headed their way. Some would never live to see the Wraith's first attack on Earth, but many would, and many would perish on the very first day.

He turned his attention upwards and watched an American Airlines, Boeing 777, fly past in the distance. Oddly, its blinking visibility lights reminded him of the swarms of delivery drones that polluted the skies of the future. Every morning on his drive into work, he would see dozens of them teeming above him. It was a little strange to see the skies here relatively empty.

"Bad dreams, huh?"

Startled, Matt spun around to see Rhea sitting on the floor with her back against the bedroom wall. She was mostly bathed in darkness, with only the glint of her left eye visible from a street light outside. "Didn't mean to startle you. Gibbons wanted me to keep an eye on you. Make sure you were OK."

Matt turned back to face his window. "Thanks."

Rhea stood and moved over to him.

She looked over at the apartment block on the opposite side of the street, every window blacked out. "Feels weird when you look out there. May as well be on another planet. I've been here nearly seven months now and still can't get used to it."

"That's comforting to know."

"You're just lucky you weren't the first person who came through."

Matt turned to her with a smirk. "Gibbons?"

Rhea nodded with a grin.

Matt turned back to his view outside. "You know, despite everything each of us went through to get here, there's a part of me that thinks... I don't know, maybe we've been given something that people in the future never had. Maybe in some strange way, coming here was good for us."

"Matt, we're not here for *us*. We're here for the future of our species." Rhea continued to watch him sit in silence by the window ledge. There was something about him - something that went beyond the physical which she found deeply attractive. Perhaps it was the hint of vulnerability he seemed to carry underneath his rugged exterior. "The dossier I read on you— said you commanded a Praetorian regiment from Alpha Corps."

"Did it mention they were also KIA under my command?"

"It did... I'm sorry, Matt. This war— it's not pretty."

"No war is," he said with a tired sigh. "What else did it say?"

"That only eight soldiers have ever escaped a Wraith enhancement facility alive. It also said, seven of those soldiers were rescued by you."

Matt sat there in silence, brooding.

Rhea knew she had just ignited some painful memories. "I didn't mean to—"

"It's OK," he said. "Technically, I didn't rescue those soldiers. At least not to begin with. I was captured for enhancement, and I merely just... broke out of prison. I made sure they tagged along for the ride."

"Yeah, about that ride. You escaped in a Death Pony?"

"Ah, huh."

"How the hell did you land it?"

"By crashing."

Rhea couldn't help but smile at that.

Matt turned to her, the steely tension coiled in his eyes softened when he returned her smile.

They both shared a chuckle.

Showered and dressed, Matt entered the kitchen later that morning to see the rest of his team gearing up for something. Everyone except Gibbons acknowledged him with a friendly nod.

"Sleep well?" Bollard asked.

"Not really," Matt replied.

"You will tonight," said Wu.

Matt grabbed a mug of fresh coffee from the kitchen and joined them.

Sprawled out across the table were five ear-bud and throat-microphones for two-way radio communication, along with mini-portable amplifiers, tablets, smartphones, chargers, and a large printed map of the D.C. Metro area.

There was also a long duffel bag underneath the table. It was zipped open. Matt caught the glint of what appeared to be a Heckler & Koch G36, with a 30-round magazine attached to it. There was also a Glock G42 protruding from the bag, which was resting on several ammo boxes of .223 NATO, and .380 ACP. Before Matt left, Adderson had given him a comprehensive briefing document on the common types of firearms used during this time. He had memorized over twenty-five assorted brands, caliber systems, and over one-hundred different models.

As Matt knelt to take a closer look, Gibbons zipped up the duffel bag and hoisted it over his shoulder. "You need to eat something. There's some cereal and fruit on the bench."

Matt watched him walk off with the duffel bag into another bedroom and close the door. He turned back to all the equipment laid out on the table. "You know, that's the one thing Adderson never told me."

"What's that?" Wu said.

"How are you paying for all of this stuff?"

Wu grinned and reached into his jacket, pulling out a thin black card with intricate gold circuitry etched into each corner. "Self-mimicking circuits. Within seconds, it can learn, replicate, and if needs be, hack any computing process. Also great for getting through firewalls and encrypted networks. This one had to be slightly modified to interface with the tech here, but we can easily tap into any cash dispensary on the street. So yeah, this little beauty right here allows us to pay for the entire show."

Matt had heard about these cards during his tour on Epsilon. He remembered a soldier who once bragged about how his older brother had acquired one on the black market, where illegal Wraith tech was sometimes sold by criminal cartels. Apparently, these particular cards used something called *self-replicating molecular code*. They were not only highly illegal, but incredibly difficult to obtain.

"I'm not gonna ask how Adderson and Cosgrove got a hold of that, but I'm guessing it wasn't cheap," said Matt.

Wu shrugged. "Chinese probably. Maybe the Russians. I've been told they can produce several a year." Wu studied the card like it was a precious artifact. "Only catch is - we can't use the same dispensary twice. We also need to keep our faces hidden, there's security cameras everywhere." Wu could see Matt's eyes were churning with more questions. He decided to get out ahead of one in particular. "And no, you don't wanna know how I got it here."

Matt cracked a tiny smile. He was starting to like Wu. There was a kind of cynicism and fatalistic humor to him that Matt appreciated. "You said cash dispensaries. People here still use paper money?"

"Some. The banks call them ATMs," Wu said. "*Automated Teller Machines.*"

"Did Adderson and Cosgrove actually bother to tell you anything before they shoved you into that conductor?" said Rhea, a firm smirk etched across her mouth.

"They told me enough. But nothing about stealing other people's money."

"We only take what we need, when we need it."

"Great, so we're *honorable* time-traveling thieves."

Wu chuckled and slipped the card back into a hidden compartment inside his jacket. "Like I said yesterday, there's a few things you'll need to get used to. Not everything we do here is going to be… you know, entirely legal."

Matt breathed a sigh and shook his head. "OK then. What about our weapons?"

"You won't get a look at them until you eat something," said Gibbons, re-entering the kitchen to open the fridge. He grabbed out a carton of whole-milk and placed it on the bench. He then opened an overhead cupboard and took out a cereal bowl, filling it with Raisin Bran. Then, he walked over and plunked the bowl down on the kitchen table, sliding out a chair, ushering for Matt to sit. "Eat."

Matt snickered. "Believe it or not, I am actually capable of getting my own breakfast."

Gibbons' face continued to hold that perpetual look of annoyance. "I'm sure you are. But I'm ordering you to sit and eat something. You haven't eaten anything substantial since you arrived. Tomorrow is a big day. You won't be of any use to me on an empty stomach."

Matt knew he was right. He took a seat. "Why, what's tomorrow?"

Gibbons moved around to the opposite side of the table and sat to face him. "Tomorrow, we make contact with Dr. Rossiter."

FORTY-SIX

CROMWELL HATED WAITING. He particularly hated waiting in this alleyway. It was filthy. Wedged behind a block of dilapidated rowhouses in Washington Heights, its grimy walls were caked in unintelligible graffiti and stunk of human urine. He shuddered to think of the potential life-threatening diseases he was exposing himself to just by standing here. But this location was well hidden from any prying eyes, which is the only reason he favored to meet his human contact here each week. It also branched off into another connecting alleyway, so if the police approached from either end, he'd have plenty of warning to disappear. However, he knew the dangers of meeting like this in broad daylight, and because of the hostile looks he received each time he ventured into this neighborhood from its denizens, he always made a point to keep his business here short.

Cromwell's human contact, P-Nut, cautiously entered the alleyway, glancing over this hunched shoulder to make sure no one was following him. He was mid-twenties, with caramel skin and a stocky build. The oversized hoodie, gold dollar sign necklace, baggy designer jeans, and sleek trainers went a long way to imply he was a lowly street dealer looking to make a name for himself quickly.

He had been running errands for Cromwell after he was approached by him with the promise of making good money on a weekly basis. And while P-Nut was more than happy at first to take his money, he was starting to have doubts about their agreement. There were several things about Cromwell's presence which always made him feel uneasy. The thick application of foundation make-up he wore, which did very little to bring life to his morose complexion, and the pale-blue eyes that were sunken deep into his skull were unsettling to look at. There was also a pungent odor that emanated from him, like a mix of rotten fruit and stale sweat.

P-Nut saw Cromwell's rail-thin form seep out from the shadows and approached with his usual jovial swagger. "What up, man?"

"Do you have what I asked for?"

"Yeah, we good, we good." P-Nut pulled out the plastic bag that was tucked underneath his hoodie. He held it open to reveal its contents.

The bag was filled with bottles of vitamins and mineral supplements; B1, B2, Niacin, as well as various antibiotics and probiotics. There was also several tubs of concealer cream and foundation.

Cromwell went to reach for the bag when P-Nut yanked it away. "Uh ah, you know the deal, man. Paper always comes first."

Cromwell handed him a rubber-banded wad of money.

P-Nut chuckled to himself as he pocketed it. There was no need to count it, he could tell by the thickness of the roll it was more than enough. "You a straight-up trip, man." He handed Cromwell the plastic bag, studying his peculiar features and icy demeanor. "You must be real sick or somethin'. Maybe it's time you go see a doctor."

Cromwell looked at him with a sullen glare and shoved the bag into his overcoat.

"It's just weird, is all I'm sayin.' I mean, I sling rock and weed, and here you are askin' me to buy make-up and all these different vitamins n' shit. No offense mister, but you a weird-ass mahfucker -

even for a white dude." P-Nut smiled at him, revealing a mouth filled with gold-plated teeth.

Cromwell did not acknowledge the smile. "You have the list for next week's supplies?"

"Yeah, I got it."

Cromwell turned and sauntered off.

P-Nut watched him for a moment, then called out after him. "Aye, yo. Hold up a sec."

Cromwell stopped and turned. "What is it?"

"Yeah see, this the thing, man. Might be a little hard to keep gettin' all this stuff each week, know what I'm sayin'?"

Cromwell stepped forward, his soulless eyes boring into P-Nut. "No, I don't know what you're saying."

P-Nut could hear the menace laced in Cromwell's voice. "Why can't you just buy them yourself online, man? None of this shit is illegal."

"I told you to never ask that question."

"Yeah, yeah, I know you actin' all like you're a secret agent or some shit."

"Online transactions are easy to trace, so that's not a viable option. You know that."

"Look man, I've been into every drug and vitamin store between here and Hill East. Even took a train out to Rockville last week. Mahfuckers are startin' to clock me. There's only so many places I can go until someone calls the cops on my ass. I'm already on parole, know what I'm sayin'?"

Cromwell took another step closer. Threateningly closer. He was almost towering over P-Nut now. "So, you're telling me you're no longer of any use to me?"

P-Nut grinned and took a step back, lifting the left corner of his hoodie to reveal the handle of the Beretta 21A Bobcat that was shoved down his jeans. "Yeah, you might wanna back the fuck up, homie."

Cromwell did not react to the sight of the gun. At least not the way P-Nut had expected. He seemed completely unphased by it.

"I think it's time you take yo creepy ass someplace else, ya feel me?"

"Saying no to me will have unfavorable consequences. Play these games all you like, but you might want to consider our initial agreement."

That agitated P-Nut even more. He drew his Beretta and aimed it directly at Cromwell's head, holding it sideways. "You think I'm playin', mahfucker? The fuck are you anyway? I don't need your paper. Got my own—"

Cromwell did not even afford P-Nut the luxury of finishing his sentence when he snatched his entire larynx out from his throat cavity.

It was so fast, it took a few seconds for P-Nut to register what had happened. His eyes went blank with shock as he gulped for air, putting a hand up to feel his throat, only to find a gaping hole of destroyed cartilage and soft tissue.

Cromwell stepped out of the way as P-Nut toppled forward like a felled tree, plowing face-first into the ground, the Beretta skittering out of his hand.

He dropped the crushed larynx next to the body. It hit the cement with a wet slap. He then picked up the Beretta, turned, and calmly walked off down the alleyway, disappearing into the chilly afternoon shadows.

FORTY-SEVEN

MATT SAT on the sofa nursing a mug of coffee, watching Wu thumb through the Bluetooth settings on his smartphone. Wu needed everyone's ear-bud and throat microphones to be synced before they left the apartment.

Gibbons, Bollard, and Rhea were in the kitchen also checking their equipment and readying themselves.

"Make sure this phone is fully charged at all times," said Wu.

"Copy that," Matt replied, checking his watch to see it was 4:35 am.

Once Matt's gear was connected to his phone, Wu handed it all to him. "I just messaged you the location of our switch car."

Matt glanced at the new text message notification on his phone. "We have a switch car?"

"If anything goes sideways out there and we have to ditch, or you get separated from us for whatever reason, we've got another vehicle parked at a lot at that address. I've also sent you the model, color, and plate number."

"Copy that," said Matt, tucking the phone into his jeans pocket.

He then stood and approached the map of Washington D.C. that was still spread out across the kitchen table, taking a moment to study the extensive street route that had been superimposed over the map in red marker. "What's our plan of attack?"

"For starters, no weapons," said Gibbons. "We're not going to war."

Matt kept his eyes on the map. He was getting sick of Gibbons treating him like an imbecile every time he asked a question. "Adderson was very clear about my need to be armed at all times."

"Adderson isn't here," said Gibbons. "Well, technically he is, but he hasn't even graduated from West Point yet."

"If I can't carry any weapons, why am I here?"

Gibbons shrugged as he threw a gray scarf around his neck. "I've been asking that question myself."

The others traded looks, unable to ignore the tension brewing between Matt and Gibbons.

Rhea was baffled as to why Gibbons had not taken to him. Like each of them, Matt had sacrificed a lot to be a part of this mission. He also presented himself as someone who was more than willing to be a team player and take direction when needed.

She joined Matt at the table, hoping she could deflate some of the tension. "Matt, we've been tracking Dr. Rossiter for the past few weeks. Fortunately, he's a creature of habit. We know his daily routine. That's been the easy part. Now we've just got to grab him off the street without any eyewitnesses, which is going to be tricky considering all his routes are exposed and heavily populated." Waiting for a response, she could see Matt was still fuming over Gibbons.

"My job here is to ensure this mission is not compromised. I can't do that if I have no way of defending us." Matt looked up at Gibbons, making sure he knew that remark was directed solely at him.

"We get that," Rhea said. "But avoiding any unwanted attention from local authorities is paramount to the success of this mission."

"You think I don't already know that?"

Gibbons scoffed. "Mr. Reeves, this is D.C. post 9/11. There's police and surveillance everywhere. This is not some Jarhead outpost on Epsilon." Gibbons then looked at Wu and Bollard and shook his head.

"You got something you wanna say to me, sir?"

"I think I've already said it."

"Then please, remind me again. Because I'm starting to think you've got a problem with me."

"You're right. I do," snapped Gibbons. "This is first and foremost a scientific expedition. I don't need some dimwitted USC grunt jeopardizing everything we've established here. It's far too important."

Bollard raised his hands in an attempt to calm the situation. "Guys, come on. Now is really not the time to be swinging dicks."

Matt was seeing red. "You know what? Fuck you, Gibbons!"

A flash of shock rippled across Gibbons' face. "Excuse me?"

"You heard. The only reason you're here is because of what I did on Epsilon - along with the millions of other *dimwitted USC grunts*. Grunts who died so you could be a part of this mission."

"I'm well aware of that."

"Really? Then what exactly are you saying?"

"I'm saying, you can't leave this apartment with a concealed weapon unless you have a very good reason to. All our firearms are unregistered. We can't risk being questioned or apprehended - especially before we make contact."

Rhea gently took a hold of Matt's arm.

He snapped to her like he'd just been electrocuted, immediately realizing how worked up he had gotten himself.

"Matt, he's right," she said. "Dr. Gibbons is just being cautious. We have to do everything possible to not jeopardize this."

There was something about Rhea's touch which calmed Matt. He liked it. He breathed deeply through his nose and nodded. Gibbons was a condescending prick, but Matt knew he was right. This was a much different time and place. There were laws he had to obey. He of all people should know how that worked.

Rhea turned to Gibbons with an unimpressed look.

Gibbons looked almost embarrassed by their confrontation. He gave her a tiny nod, then turned and headed for the front door.

Rhea then turned back to Matt. "Let's get moving. The clock's ticking."

FORTY-EIGHT

MICHAEL ROSSITER EXITED through the front door of his Brownstone apartment, dressed for his morning run.

He was tall, with an athletic build, and green-eyes that bristled with a precise mix of curiosity and warmth. In many ways, he looked more like a college football star than a scientist. At least in the stereotypical sense. Despite his academic leanings, he did in fact harbor a keen penchant for competitive sport. That came from his late father, who insisted on teaching him the principles of striving for success. For Rossiter, it was all about living by example.

His recent experimental research into antiviral therapy for Lassa Fever, and his research into linking Zika Syndrome with genetics, had garnered the attention of some very prestigious scientific bodies - both in the United States and abroad.

Of course, all of that was a cover. A smokescreen.

He couldn't talk about his real work. Not to anyone. And that was fine by him. He knew the importance of the program the Department of Defense had recruited him into - an exclusive two-year postgraduate training program in virology and epidemiology, which aside from clinical research, also held a strong focus on fieldwork. The primary mandate of this program was to deal with the prevention of the bio-threats of the future, both man-made and natural. In the interest of national security, he was set for his first trip next week; a classified field laboratory near the Panama Canal Zone. There were also other trips planned later in the year, which included Eastern Bolivia and Sierra Leone.

The small handful of the colleagues Rossiter worked alongside were all recruited into this program from various ivy-league universities, labs, and institutions around the nation. Rossiter reveled in the fact that none of his civilian colleagues knew what he really did for a living. It made him feel special. It made him feel like a secret agent.

Rossiter popped his headphone buds into each year, tapped the fitness tracker app on his phone, cued up his favorite jogging music; an eclectic mix of heavy rock and 80s New Wave pop, and took off jogging along Newport Place.

He loved the ambiance of Georgetown in the Fall. There was something about the way the sun glinted off the Federalist architecture that reminded him of the picturesque streets of Beacon Hill, in his hometown of Boston. The leafy cobblestone streets, flanked with hip cafes and fashion boutiques also added to the charm.

Since living here, Rossiter had become a bit of a foodie too, regularly enjoying the fantastic dining scene on offer. There were the usual upmarket restaurants and waterfront seafood spots you'd expect in any cosmopolitan city, but nestled in amongst them was a vibrant mix of boisterous college bars, traditional taverns, and intimate live music lounges. Georgetown had it all. This was the epicenter of his existence.

Rossiter's normal daily route would see him jog along Massachusetts Avenue, past President Woodrow Wilson House, all the way up to the Naval Observatory and back again. But today he was a little behind schedule, so he would turn around before he reached the traffic circle at Sheridan Park. On his way back, he would grab a Mochaccino from his favorite coffee bar on 22nd Street, and from there, he could easily make it home to shower for work within ten minutes.

As Rossiter paced along New Hampshire Avenue, weaving between other joggers and people walking their dogs, he could not see the black SUV that was steadily trailing behind him.

Nor could he ever imagine he was about to be kidnapped.

FORTY-NINE

MATT SAT in the back of the SUV, watching Rossiter jog along the opposite side of Massachusetts Avenue. The avenue was essentially one straight line, so they could easily shadow him while keeping their distance of around three hundred meters.

Rhea sat next to Matt, with Bollard driving and Gibbons riding shotgun. Wu had volunteered to stay behind and prep the spare bedroom for their incoming house guest. Gibbons always ensured at least one team member remained at the apartment whenever they were out in public, just in case they needed emergency assistance - or at the very worst - *extraction*.

"If we take him now, I can get him into the car before he even knows what happened," said Matt, pulling out the folded black balaclava from his jacket. Rhea also had one folded in her lap. She was going to hold the back door open while Matt grabbed Rossiter.

Gibbons shook his head, groaning with disapproval. "No, it's way too exposed. There must be at least ten foreign embassies along this avenue, each with their own security." He brought up a map of Washington D.C. on his tablet and zoomed in on a small area, holding it up for Matt and Rhea to see. "We can't grab him until he reaches the bridge at the end of this avenue. When he crosses over to head back on the opposite side, like he does every morning, we can be waiting for him. There's a small wooded area just here, between Waterside Drive and the bridge itself. We take him there, no one will see us."

As they rounded Dupont Circle, Rhea noticed Rossiter was getting smaller and smaller. "Go faster, Bollard, we're losing him."

"I'm sticking to the speed limit."

"Yeah, and you're losing him."

With no vehicles in front of them for at least another block, Bollard accelerated up to 80/mph.

But at that moment, a Metro PD patrol car was also approaching from the opposite direction. It had turned left onto Massachusetts Avenue from 21st Street and was now headed directly towards them.

Upon seeing the patrol car, Bollard pumped the brakes too hard, causing the tires to screech. Everyone jolted forward in their seats. Bollard accelerated again in an attempt to maintain some appearance of normal speed, swerving slightly across his lane.

"What the hell was that?" snapped Rhea.

"You try driving this thing," Bollard hissed at her, his eyes still fixed on the approaching patrol car.

"Relax. Just take it easy," cautioned Gibbons. "They'll pass us and keep going."

The two police officers inside the patrol car eyed the oncoming SUV. They had definitely noticed Bollard's erratic driving, and it was enough to arouse suspicion.

Matt turned his attention back on the avenue.

Rossiter was gone.

"I've lost him. He might've turned down another street," said Matt.

Rhea huffed with frustration as the patrol car passed them in the opposite lane.

Matt pivoted in his seat to watch it perform a full turn at Dupont

Circle and then merge into their lane. It was now coming up behind them, fast.

Rhea saw it too. She wheeled to Gibbons. "They're onto us. We're going to have to abort."

Gibbons' jaw was locked hard, his face riddled with dread. None of them had sufficient I.D., and what Gibbons did have was fake. Along with a stack of other fraudulent documents, he had used this I.D. to rent their apartment and purchase their smartphones. He knew the others were not holding anything illegal, but D.C. Police could still arrest them on probable cause or reasonable suspicion. They simply did not need the hassle of trying to explain who they were, and what they were doing.

"Pull over," said Matt, manually unlocking his passenger-side door.

Bollard ignored the request and continued driving, watching the accelerating patrol car gaining on them. They were approaching the traffic circle at Sheridan Park.

"We'll track him on foot." Matt shoved the balaclava back into his jacket and slipped on his sunglasses. "Quickly! Before they pull us over!"

Gibbons also continued to ignore him. He was mentally cycling through their options. There were none.

Bollard kept it just below the speed limit, gripping the steering wheel with white knuckles. His eyes flicked between the road ahead and the approaching patrol car in the rear-view mirror. "Sir, what do you want me to do?"

"Gibbons, we're gonna lose the target!" barked Matt.

Gibbons almost gasped from the tension. "OK, OK, do it! He waved his hand, signaling for Bollard to pull over. Bollard flicked his right-hand indicator on and slowed down, gently pulling into the curb.

Matt opened his passenger-side door and hopped out, careful not to look directly at the approaching patrol car.

Rhea put her sunglasses on, slid across to Matt's side and

followed him out. She closed the door and joined him, heading towards the pedestrian crossing on the corner of Massachusetts Avenue and 22nd Street.

Bollard flicked his left-hand indicator on, waiting with bated breath for the patrol car to pass them again.

It did. Slowly.

Bollard and Gibbons both remembered to breathe. Bollard then pulled out behind it and continued on along the avenue, carefully keeping his distance.

As Matt walked with Rhea, he threw a quick glance over his shoulder to see the patrol car was now pacing with them. "They're watching us. Hold my hand," he said. Rhea grabbed his hand and they continued to walk. They could hear the patrol car's engine idling alongside them. Seconds felt like hours.

Then, it suddenly accelerated past them and took off towards Sheridan Circle.

Matt and Rhea shared a relieved look. "Come on, we've gotta catch up to him."

They crossed the avenue, slow-jogging towards 22nd Street.

Once the patrol car was well out of sight, Bollard pulled over to the curb again and kept the engine running.

Gibbons tapped his smartphone and placed it on the dashboard, then pressed a finger into his throat-mic. "We'll hang back until one of you give the signal to move up."

Gibbons' voice crackled in Matt and Rhea's ears. "Copy that," Matt replied, pressing a finger against his own throat.

As they approached 22nd Street, they slowed their jog to a fast-walk. Rhea did one last scan in front and behind.

There was no sign of Rossiter anywhere on either side of the avenue.

But upon turning into 22nd Street, they immediately spotted him up ahead. He was standing outside a coffee bar, talking to a woman. Her back was to them, so they could not see her face. Her figure was tall and slim, with a mane of reddish-blond hair that was tied into a slick ponytail. The tasteful black jumpsuit and heels suggested upper-management or CEO. There was an elegance to her poise. She was someone important - perhaps on her way to breakfast with some powerful donor or lobbyist. Rossiter was relaxed while he chatted with her, indicating he knew this woman quite well.

Rhea and Matt slowed their pace to a casual stride. Matt spoke softly, never taking his eyes off the target. "We've got eyes on Rossiter again, but he's made a stop. We're gonna hang back for a moment."

Gibbons' voice crackled into their ears again. "What's he doing?"

"He's talking to a woman. Could be a neighbor or work colleague."

"Let me know when he's on the move again."

"Copy that," replied Matt.

Rhea and Matt leaned their backs against the wrought-iron fence of a condominium, lingering just next to the building's main entrance. They were at least a block away, and Rossiter had no reason to suspect he was being followed, but they still needed to be careful not to look too obvious in case he just happened to notice them watching him.

Matt's eyes narrowed while he studied the mysterious woman Rossiter was chatting with. There was something about her which seemed familiar. Maybe it was her mannerisms and her stance. He couldn't quite pin it, but it made him feel slightly uneasy.

Rossiter and the woman shared a laugh and said goodbye. He gave her a farewell wave and entered the coffee shop.

The woman turned and crossed the intersection of 22nd and P Street, continuing towards Matt and Rhea. Now facing them, they could see she was holding a takeaway coffee, with a stylish black clutch tucked under her other arm. She was out to make an impression. She was out to be noticed.

Matt studied her gait as she headed towards them. Again, it seemed familiar to him.

And then, as she drew closer, her features came into focus.

Matt's face fell as it dawned on him; she was strikingly identical to *Karen*. A spitting image of her.

Rhea caught Matt's dumbfounded expression as the woman approached. "You OK?"

Matt didn't answer her. He couldn't. He had lost the power of speech. He was paralyzed. All he could do was stand there, mouth agape as the woman passed them.

And as she did, she looked directly at Matt and gave him a tiny, almost flirtatious smile. A knowing smile.

Rhea watched her pass, then spun to Matt. "What is it?"

Matt could not peel his eyes off the woman as she walked to the end of the street, disappearing into Massachusetts Avenue.

Rhea was getting worried. Matt's face had no color left in it. She nudged him hard on the arm. "Hey! You awake?"

Matt turned to her, his eyes fixed wide with a mix of shock and bewilderment.

"Jesus, Matt, you look like you just saw a ghost."

"I— I think... I think I just did."

FIFTY

ROSSITER'S MUSIC was so loud, he could not hear the SUV roar up alongside him as he walked along 22nd Street, sipping his Mochaccino.

The black SUV screeched into the driveway of an apartment complex, blocking his path.

For a second, he wondered why the person driving was so erratic and in such a hurry. As he went to veer around the vehicle, the back door swung open and a masked man jumped out and lunged at him. He was still trying to process what was happening when a black pillowslip was thrown over his head and he was hustled into the vehicle.

Once Matt had Rossiter inside the vehicle, Rhea jumped in behind them and closed the door.

Then, the SUV reversed out of the driveway and sped off down the street.

FIFTY-ONE

AS THE BLACK SUV sped off down 22nd Street, the woman who appeared identical to Karen watched it disappear into a vein of traffic. She had witnessed the kidnapping from across the street after doubling back from where Matt and Rhea first spotted her. Everything happened just as Cromwell had predicted. Her running into Rossiter, Matt seeing her appearance, it was all part of *the plan*.

She glanced down at Rossiter's smartphone in the gutter, the earbuds were still attached to it, then bent down, picked up the phone, dropped it into her clutch, and continued on her way.

FIFTY-TWO

ROSSITER WAS in the back of the SUV, flailing and kicking so hard, Matt was struggling to zip-tie his wrists. Rhea was also grappling with Rossiter's arms, having already been hit twice in the mouth.

Rossiter continued to squeal like a stuck pig. "Help me! Someone help! Get the fuck off me!"

Matt finally managed to clamp Rossiter's wrists together and zip-tie them.

Gibbons undid his seatbelt and shifted between his seat and Bollard's to assist Matt and Rhea, putting as much weight as he could down on Rossiter's legs. Feeling another set of hands on him, Rossiter bucked even more wildly. Gibbons was worried if he wasn't subdued quickly, he'd end up kicking out a window.

Despite his wrists being bound firmly together, Rossiter wasn't calming down, so Matt decided to try a new tactic. Something a little more persuasive. He began laying into Rossiter with punches.

One connected. Something cracked. Rossiter yelped.

Gibbons reached out and grabbed Matt's arm before he could

deliver another blow. "Hey, hey! Enough! We're not trying to kill him."

Matt ignored Gibbons and thumped him again. Harder this time.

It worked. Rossiter finally stopped moving. He moaned sluggishly, his body deflating like a balloon as his head sunk into Rhea's lap. She could feel something warm and wet through her jeans. "Um... Matt, I think he's really hurt."

Matt rolled Rossiter over and ripped the black pillowcase off his head to reveal a busted nose. Blood had seeped through to Rhea's jeans.

Gibbons was furious. Matt could feel the heat from his glare, but he wasn't done yet. He grabbed Rossiter by the scruff of his running jacket and pulled him upright. "Who was that woman you were just talking to?"

Rossiter's eyes began to refocus with a mix of terror and confusion. "Who are you people? What is this?"

Matt yanked him closer. "I'm going to ask you one more time, and if you don't answer me, I'm going to start hitting you again. Who was that woman you were talking to?"

Gibbons shared a look with Rhea. "What woman?"

Rhea shrugged. "He won't tell me."

Matt tightened his grip, ready to unleash another flurry.

Rossiter got the message. "She's a friend... lives in my building."

"What's her name?"

"Karen. Her name's Karen."

Matt almost gasped. He let go of Rossiter and slumped back into his seat, the color draining from his face once again.

Battered and bloody, Rossiter looked at Rhea, Gibbons, and Bollard, his chest still heaving. He was almost beside himself. "What— what's going on here? Why have you kidnapped me? Please— someone tell me!"

Gibbons saw the look on Matt's face. He would deal with him later. But for now, he was more concerned with Rossiter's wellbeing. They needed to get off the street and back to the apartment as quickly as possible. He pivoted in his seat to face forward, slipping his seatbelt back on. "Mr. Rossiter, please forgive my colleague for that outburst. He's been under a lot of duress lately. I can assure you, it's not a method I approve of. But I do want you to know, we are not here to harm you. Actually, we wish to work with you."

Rossiter threw Gibbons an incredulous look and snorted. "You sure got a fucking odd way of interviewing people."

Gibbons grinned. He remembered a particular behavioral report he had once read about Rossiter where the author claimed his brilliance was only matched by his black-hearted wit and sarcastic sense of humor. "You are safe. And all will be explained in due course. Tell me, does your nose feel broken?"

Rossiter blinked. The adrenaline was fading. Only now could he feel the painful throb in his nose. "I— I don't know. This asshole hit me hard enough, so yeah, maybe—"

"We'll take a look once we get back," said Gibbons, trying to sound as calm and reassuring as possible.

"Where— back where?"

"I'm afraid I can't tell you that. Please, I know you're confused, but just try to relax. It won't be long now."

"Relax? I've just been kidnapped off the street."

"Think of it as... well, try and think of it as a recruitment process."

"For what?"

Gibbons turned and looked Rossiter dead in the eye. "Saving the world."

Rhea watched as Matt stared out the window in silence, watching the D.C. streets zip by. She gently reached over behind Rossiter and nudged his arm. "Hey, are you gonna tell me what the deal is with that woman you saw?"

Matt did not respond.

Rhea nudged him again. A little firmer this time. "Matt, come on. I'm being serious. Who was she?"

Finally, Matt turned and looked at her, his shell-shocked eyes fixed in a vacant stare. "My wife."

FIFTY-THREE

THE ELEVATOR DOORS OPENED, and the woman who looked identical to Karen exited onto the seventh floor of her apartment complex.

Of course, her real name wasn't Karen. That was the name Wraith Command had given her before they sent her back in time to disrupt the Emissary Program. Karen was part of a new breed of *Infiltrators;* cosmetically engineered operatives designed to look identical to the human spouses, loved ones, and colleagues of key targeted USC officials.

"Good morning, Miss Wilson," said the Concierge Doorman, who was walking towards her in the hallway. He had just assisted an elderly tenant in an adjacent apartment with her groceries. "Is there anything I can help you with?"

Karen smiled warmly at him. "I'm fine, thanks."

The Doorman gave her a polite nod and hit the call button on the elevator.

Karen entered her apartment, softly closing the door behind her.

The apartment was stylishly fitted and spacious, but aside from the single bare mattress, there was no furniture whatsoever. Flies buzzed, and maggots squirmed among the discarded, half-eaten bowls of white rice and empty vitamin bottles that littered the wooden floors.

Unlike the average Wraith, infiltrators were specifically designed to bypass many of the inherent genetic and biological defects the Wraith suffered from, but considering Earth was teeming with germs and diseases, Karen would take no chances. That's also why she chose to only eat boiled white rice. It was the one human food the Wraith could easily digest without getting violently sick. Karen knew if she were to fall ill for whatever reason, there would be no help. For the purposes of maintaining her cover, calling a doctor or visiting a hospital was simply out of the question. It would not take long for them to realize she wasn't human. As advanced as Wraith Engineers were, they were yet to create a human clone or hybrid that would be indistinguishable from the real thing.

She entered the kitchen and tossed her coffee cup into the sink. It was still full. Coffee splashed everywhere.

Karen barely mustered a glance as she opened a cupboard door and grabbed a burner cellphone out. She unlocked the screen with her fingerprint and began dialing a number.

Cromwell was standing among the hordes of morning commuters on the platform of Anacostia station when the cellphone in his overcoat buzzed.

He took it out and looked at the screen, recognizing the number. He swiped the screen and put the phone to his ear. "What is it?"

"*I have established contact. He is aware of my presence,*" Karen said on the other end of the call.

"And the scientist?"

"*He is with them.*"

"Good. Continue on." Cromwell ended the call and slipped the phone back into his overcoat.

There was a gust of wind that shot along the platform as the approaching metro train honked its horn.

Cromwell stepped forward on the platform with the other commuters, a tiny grin seeping into the corner of his cruel mouth. Everything was proceeding as he had hoped. Soon, his network would have infiltrated the Emissary Program. There would be no need for the Wraith to invade in 2048, as Earth would have already been long conquered by then.

He also looked forward to seeing Matt again. There was much unfinished business to attend to.

- END OF BOOK I -

THANK YOU FOR READING

I hope you enjoyed *The Emissary*. I also hope you'll continue the journey with Books 2, 3, and 4. Your opinion is very important, so please take a moment to leave a short review on Amazon. A star-rating with a quick word or two can make a big difference. It will also help other like-minded readers discover my books.

Until next time, happy reading.

Cheers,
Terrance

ABOUT THE AUTHOR

Terrance resides in Queensland, Australia, with his wife and two dogs. When he's not busy fending off hordes of radioactive Kangaroos and flesh-eating Wombats, he can usually be found lurking around his office, conjuring his next book idea.

For more information please visit:
TerranceMulloyAuthor.com

Made in United States
Orlando, FL
03 April 2022